Jane wore all black. Or rather, the black wore her.

Displayed her. Intimately. Right down to the hot-pink hoochie-mama sandals on her feet.

Dazed, Dom focused on her hot-pink toenails, and then ran his gaze up every luscious curve to her hot-pink siren's lips. *Say something.* The message flashed to his muddled brain. "You're late."

Her chin rose. "Yes. You have a problem with that?"

He slowly shook his head. His eyes moved from her lips to her breasts: gifts from the gods, cruelly covered.

He lurched helplessly on his bar stool and forced his curiously rubbery legs to the ground. Dom peeled his dry lips apart. "You're dressed to kill."

Her mouth curved. "It's appropriate for the occasion."

*Oh man, oh m*__ *purpose!* As so__ was boss and to__ come back apo__ him badly enou__

Dom grinned, displaying every tooth he owned, feeling in__ __ "Well, then. Let's get this gam__

Dear Reader,

Have you ever found yourself thinking, "That guy would be perfect if only…"? Maybe it's his attitude. Maybe it's his clothes or his posture. Maybe it's his table manners. Something stops him from being that man of your dreams.

Well, I sure have! And in this world of being able to upgrade a flight to first class, a room to ocean view, or your wardrobe to fabulous – I wondered, wouldn't it be great if we could also upgrade our men?

That's how I came up with the concept behind my new miniseries, THE MAN-HANDLERS – women who make over their men. *Who's on Top?* is the story of lovable control freak Jane O'Toole and alpha male Dominic Sayers, two incredibly strong-willed people who are each determined to best the other. Watch as the sexual sparks between them blaze a trail from the office to the bedroom! And place your bets on the winner. You'll be the final judge of who's on top! I hope you enjoy getting to know Jane and Dom as much as I enjoyed creating them.

And I love to hear from readers! Visit me at my website at www.KarenKendall.com, where you can enter my monthly contest and find information about upcoming releases.

Happy reading!

Karen Kendall

PS – Look for the next book in the series, *Unzipped?*, coming in August 2006!

WHO'S ON TOP?

BY
KAREN KENDALL

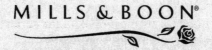

MILLS & BOON®

To my husband, Don, who has resisted most of my attempts to upgrade him – because, of course, he is perfect! And to my wonderful editor, Wanda Ottewell. Thanks for everything.

First published in Great Britain 2006
by Harlequin Mills & Boon Limited, Eton House,
18-24 Paradise Road,
Richmond, Surrey TW9 1SR

© Karen Moser 2005

ISBN-13: 978 0 263 84605 8
ISBN-10: 0 263 84605 9

14-0706

Printed and bound in Spain
by Litografía Rosés S.A., Barcelona

1

IF ONLY MONDAY WERE A HOT, half-naked man, I wouldn't mind starting every week with it. Jane O'Toole yawned.

Whether you're a sanitation worker or a CEO—or in my case, both—Mondays just...suck.

She emptied the last wastebasket into the trash bag, tied a knot into the top of the bag and set it outside the office door, breathing deeply of the crisp October air.

Farmington, Connecticut, was at its most beautiful in autumn, nestling among the fall foliage under royal-blue skies. A town of twenty-one thousand, Farmington personified New England, abundant with neat Cape Cods punctuated with maple, oak and elm trees. Window boxes hadn't yet lost their colorful blooms to the winter, and the wind sang through leaves of spectacular gold, rich tawny cinnamon, eggplant and even burgundy.

Such a gorgeous day to be stuck in the office. She left the door open to let the sunshine in, bathing the room and its antique-reproduction furniture in gold. Wryly Jane noted that the light also illuminated every dust mote stuck to the dark wood. And the once-pristine arrangement of dried roses on the coffee table looked…hairy.

Is it possible to dust dried flowers? she wondered. If she blew on them, she'd sneeze. If she vacuumed them, she'd be left with headless stems. And surely the duster in the closet would only add blue feathers to the unappetizing hair.

Jane dreamed of a cleaning service one day, but the business was too fragile, too new, to justify the expense right now. She'd conceived Finesse a year ago, while working at her miserable job in corporate employee assistance. Her M.A. in psychology had qualified her to be a glorified babysitter and paper pusher, and after eight years she'd had enough. So had her friends Shannon Shane, a would-be actress, and Lilia London, who'd been a receptionist for a law firm.

Jane had envisioned a business of their own: a training center for personal and career enhancement. Open now for nine months, Finesse did consulting on employee management issues and some general counseling (Jane's specialty), image/communication (Shannon's) and business etiquette (Lilia's).

Thanks to hard work and tireless marketing, they'd enjoyed great success so far—though like any business in its fledgling stage, they had loans to pay off. And salaries? Actual salaries for each of them were still a dream on the horizon.

Jane put off donning those snappy pink rubber gloves and heading for the bathroom. *Ugh.* She'd do it *after* she had a doughnut.

She listened with half an ear to Shannon and Lilia discuss the pros and cons of…thong underwear? Yes, she had heard right.

"I don't see how you can stand it," Lilia said to Shannon with a shudder. Lilia's dark hair was demure, as usual, clamped at her neck with a conservative clip. In her well-cut gray silk suit, she looked every inch the etiquette consultant.

Shannon marched to an altogether different drummer. In fact, Jane was pretty sure she had an alternate orchestra. She didn't look anything like an image consultant—unless it was for rock stars in L.A.

"A thong eliminates the pantie-line problem." Shannon shrugged, winding her long, curly blond hair into a knot on her head. Her motorcycle jacket hid most of a screaming-orange tank top—just not enough of it for Jane's taste.

"I haven't tried them," Lilia said, "but I've heard those new boy shorts hide pantie lines, too."

"Nope—they crawl." Shannon was indisputably the authority on undies.

"Better a little 'crawl' than…than…rope burn in a private place!" Lilia stood her ground.

"Thongs are really not uncomfortable," said Shannon. "The only problem I have with them is that I'm forever putting them on sideways, since they're your basic isosceles triangle."

Lilia shook her head. "Never. I just can't go there. Thongs are so…slutty."

Shannon exchanged a glance with Jane and both started to laugh.

"Ah," Jane responded in a dry voice. "It's so much *less* slutty to wear *nothing* under your stockings, for fear of those dreaded pantie lines."

Lilia colored. "That's not the same thing at all—"

"No," Shannon chortled in between mouthfuls of a Krispy Kreme doughnut. "It's worse! Lilia, you fallen woman, you." She turned to Jane. "Now, execu-babe, tell us all about *your* unmentionables."

Jane grinned, dried her just-washed hands and helped herself to what was left of the Krispy Kremes. "The only thing you need to know about my underwear has to do with maintenance. You go into Vicky's Secret, and let's say you choose beautiful lace tap pants. Or some sheer panties in chiffon. You feel pretty the first time you wear them. Then you toss them into the washing machine—'

"You didn't!" gasped Lilia. "Surely the salesgirls told you to hand wash—"

"Yes, like I have all the time in the world to gently swish each of my freakin' undergarments in the sink. Get real."

Lilia tsk-tsked.

"So I threw them into the machine. And now they're wound around the bottom of the post thingy in the washer and I can't get them out! I'm also afraid to use the darn machine in case they destroy it or set it on fire or something."

Shannon laughed.

Lilia stated the obvious. "You should call a repair guy."

"Sure, Lil. *You* try explaining to a guy your father's age that the problem lies with your ruby-red lacy tap pants. That it's going to take a blowtorch and some needle-nose pliers to get them unstuck."

Lilia's lips twitched.

Jane mock-glared at her friends before rounding on Shannon. "By the way, thanks for leaving me only the squashed glazed doughnut and significantly less than half of the chocolate-frosted one!"

Shannon rolled her eyes. "I have two adages for you. 'First come, first served.' And 'It's for your own good, honey.' Be glad they're on my hips and not yours."

"Why?" Jane muttered. "*Why* have I maintained a twenty-year friendship with the two of you? Not to mention going into business with you. Next Monday I'll eat all the crème ones before reaching the first traffic light, and you'll be sorry you treated me this way."

Lilia said, "Now, girls."

Shannon stuck her tongue out.

"Speaking of panties and Vicky's Secret," Jane went on, stalking to the prissy camelback sofa and retrieving a catalogue. "How on earth is anyone supposed to wear—" she flipped through some pages "—*this?* It's only got a—"

Suddenly Shannon made a weird face, rolling her eyes wildly, and Lilia coughed and waggled her index finger behind her ear.

"—string of pearls for a crotch!" Too late she noticed their odd expressions.

Both her business partners closed their eyes and winced.

Slowly Jane lowered the catalogue and looked gingerly behind her, only to behold a Hugh Jackman type in pinstripes—her first client of the day. *Oh. My. God.* His shoulders filled the doorway and he gazed down at her from a height of at least six foot two. His dark hair was cut short in an attempt to restrain a tendency to curl. Dark eyes gleamed at her over Serengeti shades that he'd tugged down just a bit. Besides his suit, he wore a quizzical expression, and his eyebrows formed two interested, sex-charged squiggles.

She cleared her throat; resisted putting her hands up to her incinerated cheeks; looked at her watch. "You must be Mr. Sayers. I wasn't expecting you… quite so early."

DOMINIC SAYERS FROZE IN HIS tracks. *String of pearls for a crotch?* The concept was undeniably appealing—he was only human, after all. But he could not possibly be in the right place. Had he stumbled into an upscale escort service? He took a step back; looked up at the discreet, silver wooden letters. *Huh.* He raised a brow and returned his gaze to the rosy cheeks of the woman before him.

"Jane O'Toole? Of…Finesse?" He didn't try to conceal his irony.

The color in her cheeks deepened to burgundy, but

other than that she didn't bat an eyelash. He was, however, too irritated to admire her composure. He didn't want to be here.

"Yes, that's right." She raised her chin and stuck out her right hand. "A pleasure to meet you, Mr. Sayers."

"Oh, I doubt it." His gaze, which he'd meant to keep cool and distant, roved over her body without his permission, dipping into the neatly buttoned but still provocative valley where the plackets of her blouse met—and downward from there. Hmm, pearls…

She blinked. "If you'd like to have a seat, I'll get you started on some paperwork. Just some simple questions. Your employee ID number for Zantyne Pharmaceuticals, their billing address—that type of thing."

"Ah, yes. The paper trail," he said, returning to reality and not bothering to hide his bitterness. But he sat and accepted the pen and file folder she handed to him.

Arianna "the piranha" DuBose was no doubt furiously adding as much as she could to the paper trail that would indicate he should be fired.

The trail would not include certain important information: that Arianna had lied, backstabbed and schmoozed her way into her current position as his boss; that she was extremely threatened by Dom and didn't want him around to expose her or show her up; and that she'd deliberately picked a fight with him so she could get him some "help" for his "negative attitude" and "tendencies toward insubordination."

He shouldn't have fallen for her tricks. Damn it, he *knew* better. What had gotten into him? Why had he let her anger him? And why hadn't he made sure someone else was in the room during the entire standoff?

The only blessing Dom could count was that Arianna-the-piranha hadn't accused him of sexual harassment.

Still, he was here in Jane O'Toole's office to be evaluated—probably to commence "sensitivity training," anger management and who knew what else. General kowtowing, he supposed.

In the meantime, he had a market analysis due, the regulators breathing down his neck and the licensing agreements to sign off on. Arianna would be nosing around every step of the way, erasing the dots from his i's and smudging the crosses on his t's. Anything she could use to trump up a case against him—she'd latch on to it with those flesh-eating fangs of hers.

Dom realized that Jane O'Toole was saying something to him. "What?" he asked gruffly. "I didn't catch that."

His eyes went from her mouth to her neckline, where she was fidgeting with—hoo, boy—a string of pearls. Again his male radar perked up. *Hmm...*

As soon as she followed his gaze, she dropped them as if they were hot.

He lifted a corner of his mouth. He didn't mean it as a sneer exactly, but she seemed to take it as one, since she stiffened.

She was extremely attractive, with a mess of dark curly hair. This was cut at a sensible chin length and offset by huge brown eyes. Her cheekbones weren't high but soft and rounded, blending into a surprisingly strong square chin.

She had plenty of interesting curves, too, though they were mostly hidden by a dark green pantsuit. He had a suspicion that lush, heavy breasts nestled against the lucky lining of her jacket. If Dom had met her in a bar—not that he usually went to bars, except to play pool—well, hell, he might have stiffened, too. So to speak.

His eyes strayed once again to the pearls at her neck, and he fought off an image of them in a darker, duskier place—attached to a scrap of silk.

"I asked you if you'd like a *cup of coffee,* Mr. Sayers." The flush in her cheeks had spread down to her neck now, providing an interesting background for her pearls.

"Coffee would be great," he said. He accepted it with thanks, omitting sugar or cream. He focused on the hot, black stuff and not Jane O'Toole's possible tastes in lingerie. *Grow up, Sayers.* But hell, he felt all of thirteen, having been sent to the principal's office.

Ms. O'Toole mixed her own coffee with as many cancer-causing substances as she could scrape together and stirred the disgusting brew with a long stick, which she tossed into the trash. "Why don't we go into my office?"

The other two women involved in the kinky undies discussion—a six-foot Harley babe and a prim china doll—had vanished behind their respective doors. Dom shrugged and followed Principal O'Toole into her den of discipline. They might as well get on with his knuckle rapping.

"Have a seat," she told him. She walked to a filing cabinet and bent over the second drawer, retrieving a sheet of paper from a manila folder. "This is a permission form—I always videotape my first session with a client. Then I'll make a couple of tapes midway through our course together and one during the very last meeting. It's just to document progress. I don't release them to anyone, under any circumstances. But I do need you to sign off on the form."

Dom folded his arms across his chest and told her he didn't like the idea at all.

"Why not?" she asked calmly. "Is there something about being taped that threatens you?"

"No, Ms. O'Toole. I don't feel threatened. But I would like to discuss a few issues with you and I don't necessarily want them on record."

She sat in her cushy leather chair opposite him and crossed her legs. Then she folded her hands across a leather-bound notebook in her lap. A pen emerged from the bundle of fingers, punctuating her air of cool disapproval like an exclamation point. Damn Arianna. He'd already been tried, judged and found lacking. But all Jane O'Toole said was, "Fine."

"I want you to know that I'm not a behavioral problem," he said. He could hear the anger in his own voice; saw her note it. "I do not have insubordination issues. I am not a chauvinist jerk who is unable to work for a woman. Is that clear?"

"Crystal," she said. "So now that you've told me what you're *not,* how about telling me what you *are?*"

"I'm a red-blooded American guy who doesn't enjoy being manipulated by a power-hungry bitch."

Her jaw dropped open and he heard her teeth click together as she shut it. *Gotcha.*

"Mr. Sayers, I've been called a lot of things during the course of my career, but that is a first."

"I meant Arianna DuBose, not you!"

"I'm relieved to hear it. So tell me more about your working relationship with Ms. DuBose."

A nice open-ended question. Gave him lots of rope to hang himself. Well, what the hell. He already had. "Ms. DuBose is an ambitious sociopath, and I happened to get in her way."

"I see."

"No, I don't think you do. I was in line for a promotion and should have been a shoo-in. Suddenly the other regional managers were eyeing me uneasily, and Arianna got the job. Now she's got it in for me. She wants me gone."

Jane O'Toole took a careful sip of coffee and set her cup down on a side table. She uncrossed and recrossed her legs, unconsciously exhibiting lean, muscular calves. "So you're battling a certain resentment that Ms. DuBose was promoted ahead of you. I can see how that would make you angry."

She didn't believe him. Of course she didn't. It all sounded like sour grapes to his own ears. And paranoid, to boot. Dom felt tension growing in every muscle, fresh anger seeping through his veins. Arianna had him just where she wanted him: by the short and curlies. But by God, he wasn't going to let her win. He had to get through to this O'Toole woman.

Charm. Where had his charm gone hiding? He almost growled out loud. Due to the sheer injustice of the situation, his charm had been squished beneath his heel like an old piece of gum. But he'd better figure out how to scrape some off and resurrect it into a nice big pink bubble, or Jane would unwittingly help Arianna destroy his career.

Ugh. The harder Dom thought about charm, the more it eluded him. He *was* mad, damn it. Justifiably so. And worse, he was embarrassed. How dare Arianna send him to this woman, like a rowdy child in need of a paddling?

He got up out of his chair and paced Jane's office a couple of times. She just watched him out of those brown eyes, schooled carefully to be dispassionate. But he could sense her judgment, and it wounded his pride.

"Ms. O'Toole, it's very clear to me that you think I'm a swine."

The lashes fluttered over those baby browns and she bit her lip. "No, of course not."

He snorted, walked back to the chair he'd been sitting in and pounded the back of it with his fist. "Come off it. You think I'm a pig."

She raised a brow. "Your choice of words, not mine."

Dom bared his teeth at her. "And you're right. I am angry. But not for the reasons you think. However, I'm too irate to discuss all of this with you at the moment, so I'm going to put an end to our session." He turned on his heel, walked to the door and opened it.

Jane sat in her chair and made a couple of notes. Then she got up and followed him to where he was standing gazing down at the catalogue she'd tossed on the sofa by the door. He was unable to look away from the tiny silk G-strings available in hot-pink or midnight-black, the ones with the—

He heard the click as she clutched at her necklace. Turned to see the red flash into her cheeks once again. He raised a brow, knowing that he shouldn't voice the words even as he said them. "It's always best…not to dangle pearls before swine, Ms. O'Toole."

JANE REACHED HER LIMIT WITH this comment. She banished the blush from her cheeks and removed her hand from her necklace. "No one dangled anything in front of you, Mr. Sayers. You rooted out the mud all by yourself. And it's clear to me that you're trying to knock me off balance so that I'll let you run away."

He froze. The faint devilry and arrogance that had risen with his mocking eyebrows disappeared, and his lips flattened. "Run away?"

She nodded and continued on the offensive. "As fast as you can get your snout out the door." It was the only way to get him back into her office and address the issues at hand.

Sayers's shoulders seemed to grow wider and a definite glint shone in his eye. "I don't run from anything, Jane O'Toole. Not sociopathic bosses and not smug little psych majors with an ambition to fix what *ain't broke*. Understand?"

Oh, but I will fix you, Mr. Attitude. You just don't know it yet. All men need to be fixed! "Yes, Dominic Sayers, I believe I do. Now, since we've established that you're not running away, let's step back into my office—shall we?" *Ha! I've got you now.*

His eyes narrowed. He couldn't walk out the door and still retain any self-respect. And he knew it. She restrained a smile. Was it her imagination or did every faint pinstripe on the man's suit indicate a bullet trajectory—all of them aimed right at her?

Jane smiled at his back as he stalked once again toward her office. Hostility and annoyance buzzed around them like a thousand angry horseflies.

She dropped into her chair and made a couple more notes. This made her look official and professional and gave her a moment to think. *Continue on the offensive,* she told herself. *Just take the bull by the horns. Maybe that way he'll smash some excellent psychological china....*

"So, Mr. Sayers. How long *have* you entertained hostile thoughts toward women? Does this date back to your childhood?"

He fixed her with an extremely black, dangerous

stare—and then he began to curse. She ignored the actual words and just let him vent. But in the meantime she couldn't help but admire the way he filled out his suit, the jump of the muscles in his stern jaw as he got pithy with her and the truly miraculous bone structure of his face. The man had cheekbones that would make a sculptor weep.

When he finally stopped with an insult to her profession, she said graciously, "I'm so glad we've had this time together," and opened her appointment book. "I'd like to visit you at the office on Monday, all right? Nine-ish, shall we say?"

Sayers appeared to choke on that breath he was taking. "Lady, are you out of your mind?"

"No, I'm certainly not. Let's identify what just happened here. Since you were too proud to walk out that door, when I asked you a question you resented, you exhibited enough hostility that you hoped I'd be horrified and back out of working with you. I'm not going to do that. Of course, again it's your choice. You can retreat from the battlefield and refuse to work with *me*." She watched him carefully for a moment. "But then I'll have to log that in my evaluation. And if what you say about the, uh, *sociopathic* Ms. DuBose is true, then won't you just be playing into her hands?"

2

By the time Dominic Sayers left her office, Jane was smug in the knowledge that she'd won the round. Oh, yes indeed—he was down for the count, with her high heel firmly planted between his handsome shoulder blades. It was a darn good feeling—but she couldn't help questioning how long it would last. Dominic would be armed and dangerous next time they met. She had to prepare herself. And she had to get him to talk to her.

Besides being angry, who was this man? She didn't have many clues. And if she couldn't figure out who he was, how was she going to figure out how to fix him?

She stared at the obnoxious, broad, dark back of Sayers as he walked to his hunter-green Jaguar and unlocked it. The guy didn't saunter exactly. He just walked casually, with confidence radiating off what she had to admit were exceptionally nice shoulders. She wondered fleetingly what he looked like in a snug T-shirt before her gaze dropped to his backside, which was so fine that she could watch it like a television. She wouldn't be at all surprised if strange women pinched it on the street….

That's when he caught her, acknowledging her stare with one of his own.

Annoyed at herself, she turned on her heel, only to have her gaze fall on the glossy Vicky's Secret catalogue that had launched some of the trouble between them. Because there *was* trouble between them, no doubt about it—layers of disturbance that had to do not only with a battle of wits but also with an underlying resistance to each other. Jane didn't like this one bit. Because the flip side of resistance was…*attraction.*

How could she be attracted to a foul-mouthed self-professed swine? Well, truth to tell, he was more of a grizzly bear.

Jane had always loved a good fight. And she usually won—just as she had today. But she *was* attracted to Sayers, God help her.

Ugh. There it was, lying out in the open for her to deal with. But how?

She snatched the offending lingerie catalogue off the sofa and stuffed it into the nearest circular file.

The planet was littered with Vicky's Secret catalogues. Bombarded with bras, plastered with panties. She was so used to seeing them, modeled by half-naked nymphets, that she hadn't thought to hide the damned catalogue in the depths of the cleaning closet.

And out of all the possible selections in such a catalogue, Mr. Sayers had to have caught her looking at *that* one. Jane clutched the pearls at her neck and let her fingers slide along the smooth orbs, trying not to imagine how they might feel slithering into dark, sensual crevices. She shifted from one foot to the other, feeling heat blossom on her skin at an unbidden image of Sayers trailing his fingers after them....

Then she slapped herself in the forehead. What was *wrong* with her? Jane stuck her foot in the wastebasket and stomped on the damn catalogue just to make herself feel better.

Shannon's door opened behind her. "Now *that's* a good look for you, O'Toole."

With dignity, Jane removed her foot from the container.

"Almost as good a look as the beet-red on your face an hour ago."

Jane shot her a look that communicated two words: *bite me.*

"So what's up with him, and why do you look like you just ate a nail sandwich?"

Jane sighed. "He doesn't want to be here. Remember how thrilled I was to hear from that female VP? The one from Zantyne?"

Shannon nodded.

"Well, she's the one who sent Mr. Sunshine this morning. And he *does* seem to have an attitude problem. He's going to be a tough client."

"Not to mention a hot one!"

Jane ignored the comment completely, as well as the smirk on her friend's face.

"But if you do well with him," Shannon guessed, "we could get a lot more business from Zantyne—business that we need if we want to break even this year, service the business loans and hire a receptionist."

"Exactly."

Shannon tapped a long fingernail against her teeth. The fingernail was purple. Yesterday it had been blue.

"Hey, Shan? Your nails aren't going to be green tomorrow, are they? I mean, we—"

"Have a corporate image to uphold, yes, I know. Trust me, once I have my first clients in here next week, the claws will be short and neutral. But until then I'm a free spirit, honey. And green's not a bad idea…MAC has a new metallic mint color out. Thanks for reminding me."

Jane looked down at Shannon's toes, which gleamed—alternately striped and polka-dotted with silver and purple. She shook her head. "Where do you find the time?"

"Exactly where you find the time to run on your treadmill like a gerbil on a wheel. Back to this hunky guy with the eyebrows. Convince him that he can use you for his own purposes, and then he'll relax."

Jane nodded slowly, trying to ignore the dirtier connotations of being used for Sayers's own purposes. *Stop that! He's a client.*

Shannon might have a few nuts in her center, but she was often unexpectedly brilliant. "I think you're right," Jane said in her best crisp and professional tones. "He's not the kind of personality who will accept help. He needs to be in control."

Shannon smirked. "Hmm. Kind of like some other people I know…"

"Hey, it's not my fault I'm a Virgo. I was born that way."

"No, I think you dictated the exact date and time you exited the womb. You also took notes, cc-ing the doctor and your parents."

Jane was smart enough to check the door this time for roving clients before shooting the finger at Shannon. Oh, yes, she had Finesse.

SHE WAS DRAWN BACK INTO HER office by the ringing phone and she could still smell Dominic Sayers's scent as she picked up the receiver. "Jane O'Toole."

"Hi, honey."

Her heart turned over at the sound of her father's voice, monotone and depressed, as he was most of the time. She worried about him constantly. "Hey, Dad. What's up?"

"Gilbey got himself fired again. Don't know what to do with that boy."

Jane plopped into her leather chair, squishing all the air out of the seat cushion in an indelicate *whoosh*. She slipped off one brown leather pump and rubbed the arch of her bare foot against the toe of the other. "What happened this time?"

"Some BS about how the foreman doesn't like him, wrote him up for being a minute late, yada yada."

She'd heard it all before—many times—which was probably why she was allergic to the blame game. Her brother Gilbey, just like Dominic Sayers today, always had a boss who was out to get him. And conveniently for Gilbey, the boss always did. Then Gil didn't have to work while he "searched" for his next job. It was all very convenient. Jane sighed.

"Dad, he's not going to grow up if you don't kick him out of the house. He's going to remain mentally seventeen forever—and he's twice that age!"

Her father muttered something.

"You know I'm right. Do you want me to talk to him again?"

"Can't hurt. And maybe you can help line him up some other prospects."

"No." Her voice was firm. "I can't recommend him to anyone when I know what he's like."

"He's your brother, Janey."

"Yes! He's my brother, and therefore my own reputation is on the line when I put in a good word for him. It's embarrassing when he gets fired."

"Just promise me you'll think about it."

I am thinking about it. That's why I'm slowly going insane. "So how are you doing, Dad? Are you cheering up a little?"

"Well, you know. Darn weeds keep growing in the walkway, no matter what I put on 'em. Got moles in the front lawn. And the Jets are gonna get the snot kicked out of them tonight, you mark my words."

"I'll bet the hardware store has something to take care of the weeds and moles. I can't help you much with your team, though. You just might have to pick a different one."

"I'm no fair-weather fan, Janey. I stick with my boys!"

I know, and your loyalty is one of the things I love most about you. But judging by their current stats, that means you're going to be depressed until basketball season starts up.

She didn't say it aloud. "Why don't you get out into the sunshine and take a walk, Dad? It'll make you feel better." *And how about some nice Prozac?*

"Unnh."

"Really."

"Unnh."

Well, this is progress. "What would you like me to bring for dinner on Sunday?"

"Unnh."

"Meat loaf? With mashed potatoes and peas?"

"Unnh."

Jane decided he'd answered in the affirmative. "Okay, then. I'll see you Sunday."

She placed the receiver back in its cradle, and her thoughts returned to Dominic Sayers. Unfortunately the thoughts were not of a professional nature: he was shirtless, displaying a tan, six-pack abs and a wicked grin. He was also beckoning her to come sit on his lap—which she did very happily, disengaging his buckle, pulling off his belt and using the leather to strap him to the chair he sat in. Then she—

Jane O'Toole, get a grip on yourself! You've obviously been working too hard and are in desperate need of a date.

She tried to remember how long it had been and then decided she didn't want to think about that.

Wiping her mind clean, she opened a new file on her laptop and stared at the blinking cursor for a moment before typing in his name. Under it she wrote:

Attitude problem. Bullheaded. Seems to thrive on confrontation. Blames others (boss) for current predicament. Arrogant. Aware of physical attractiveness. Competitive streak several miles wide.

Treatment plan:

1. Exploit and then control subject's hostility; get him to relax and open up.

2. Establish more about subject's background. Does he have an underlying anger at women?

3. Observe subject in office environment. Gather examples to show him how his behavior negatively impacts his relations with co-workers. Pay special attention to interaction with females.

4. Bring up these examples in a nonthreatening way and explore alternate scenarios for subject to employ next time.

5. Using the above examples, get subject to
admit he has a problem and that he can solve it.
6. Do not allow subject's looks or your own libido to sway you from your objectives!

Jane stared at the computer screen. Now where
had number six come from? She needed to remember that Sayers was not a nice guy. He had likened
himself to a pig.

That scent of his wasn't at all porcine, though—
woodsy, male, a hint of clove—and it still hung in her
office. Jane spun in her chair to face the credenza,
from which she pulled a can of Lysol. She depressed
the nozzle and walked it around the room on full blast.

*Take that, Sayers. I'll figure you out. And then I'll
fix you like a bad habit.*

SUNDAY DINNER WAS ITS USUAL barrel of laughs. How
could you love two people so much and be so frustrated by them? Jane reminded herself that even a
graduate degree in psychology couldn't answer a
question like that.

"The potatoes are dry," her dad muttered. Gilbey
said nothing as he helped himself to a slab of meat
loaf, placing it in the center of a lake of ketchup on
his plate.

Jane contemplated what this said about her
brother as she methodically scraped her father's portion of mashed potatoes back into the serving bowl
and added butter and cream. As she reached into a

cabinet for the electric beaters, her dad said, "Now don't make 'em too fattening, Janey."

She plugged the beaters in. "Adding water won't make them taste very good." The noise drowned out any possible response from her dour dad. When she was done, Jane scooped a healthy portion of mashed potatoes back onto his plate and watched with satisfaction as he began to eat them with obvious enjoyment—not that he could allow himself to acknowledge it.

"Probably'll gain five pounds," he groused between bites.

She just smiled. He was on the skinny side and had abnormally low cholesterol. She wasn't worried.

Her gaze returned to Gilbey, who was now turning his plate to make sure the meat loaf was truly centered in the ketchup. "Perfect," he announced to nobody in particular.

Did he want a compliment for his skill? "You know, Gil, most people put the meat loaf on the plate first and then the ketchup on top."

"I'm not most people."

Truer words had never been spoken.

"Why do you do it that way?"

"Because it works better."

Jane shook her head, but as she watched him eat, she was struck by the fact that it *did* work better—at least for him. Gil had a hard time with accepted structure. He was always questioning traditional ways of doing things. She'd called him stubborn and exasperating many times. But maybe he was just creative.

Gilbey, in his own way, was as unique as Shannon. But if Shannon marched to an alternate orchestra, Gil shambled along to an alternate grunge band.

Jane stuck a piece of meat loaf into her own mouth and tried to catch her brother's gaze, but he wouldn't look at her. He was ashamed at the loss of another job. Well, he should be, darn it!

"Your critical side is not your most attractive side," she heard her mother say in her head. Jane all but rolled her eyes. *Yeah, but you can't be blind to people's faults, either.*

She fought against her judgmental side, she really did. She used it to *help* people, to fix their problems. She was good at that. She'd founded a company to do it. Her critical side would end up being her most lucrative side. Most companies steadily lost money for the first three years they were in business. Thanks to her, Finesse was close to breaking even in nine months.

Jane's thoughts turned to her mother again, now dead of breast cancer twelve years. Mom would never have bought meat loaf and mashed potatoes. She'd have made them—and not the powdered kind either, as Jane suspected these were.

Dad hadn't been surly and depressed when she was alive, and Gilbey hadn't been quite such a mess—she'd had him doing all kinds of landscaping for her, even building a rock waterfall by hand. Jane still remembered him then, totally absorbed in his task, working twelve hours a day with only a twenty-minute lunch break. Gilbey loved to work with his hands. She understood that.

That's why the last three jobs she'd gotten him had involved manual labor. But he'd walked off the construction job, put all the parts together backward on the assembly-line job and butted heads with the foreman on this latest one, a position in an electronics company.

What am I going to do with you, Gil? It simply never occurred to her that he wasn't her problem.

On the other side of the table, her dad put down his fork and rubbed his belly. "Feel like I swallowed a bowling ball."

"Did you enjoy the meal, Dad?"

"Unnh." But he nodded.

She picked up his plate and wished that men of his generation would acknowledge the arrival of feminism and do their own dishes. Yeah, right. Dad would clean up the kitchen the same day he mowed the lawn *en pointe,* in a pink ballerina tutu.

In that one regard, it was a good thing that Gilbey still lived with him. Jane took the plates to the sink and rinsed them. To the mental list in her head she added: antidepressants for Dad, another job for Gilbey. The men in her life always needed help.

That night, to her shame, Jane dreamed of a hot, naked Dominic Sayers who needed help finding his clothes. Funny, but she refused to give them to him.

In fact, she had hidden them herself and she taunted him with a single sock…for which Dominic had to chase her down. Laughing, he pinned her against the wall and demanded his things, threatening to take hers if she didn't return them.

When she refused, he opened her blouse with his teeth, scattering buttons across her bedroom floor. Next he pulled down her bra, wedging it under her breasts and taking the nipples into his mouth.

Jane moaned and tried to free her hands, but he wouldn't let her go—just captured both her wrists in his right hand and pulled up her skirt with his left. Then his fingers crept under her panties, skimming over hidden curls and caressing, teasing, rubbing her most secret places. He cupped her with a warm palm and slid back and forth, back and forth….

Jane shuddered, gasped for breath and awoke disoriented, breathing heavily. It was dark. The clock read 3:33 a.m., and her body vibrated with—no other word for it—horniness. She ached with lust. Her brain felt foggy. And no way in hell would she fall back asleep before dawn. Crazy though it was, she'd inhaled Dominic Sayers like a virulent flu. Would she recover anytime soon?

3

JANE STOOD IN HER OFFICE, hands on her hips, in front of the hairy flower arrangement. There *had* to be a way to dust the darn thing without making it disintegrate. The coffee was brewing, and this was her challenge of the moment—the one she felt she could triumph over before having to follow the annoyingly sexy, butt-headed Dominic Sayers around his office like a Labrador retriever. Well, a Lab with opposable thumbs, a notepad and a definite agenda.

She went to the closet that held cleaning supplies and stood there looking at the array of possibilities for cleaning flowers. Furniture polish? Soft soap? Disinfectant spray? Nope. And she'd already ruled out the vacuum. Could she swish the flower heads around in the toilet? *I don't think so.*

Finally her gaze settled on a mini fan, which she pulled out and set on the floor near the offending arrangement. She plugged it in, turned it on and aimed it satisfactorily. The flowers began to rattle in the breeze, and a gazillion dust motes swirled into the air in a mini tornado. There!

The door opened to admit Lilia, who took one look and assumed an expression of kindly tolerance for the insane.

"Did you bring doughnuts?" Jane asked hopefully.

"Of course. I have a dozen in my four-by-six inch pocketbook."

The article in question was a little quilted number that hung from Lilia's shoulder by a thin gold chain. Definitely no edibles in there, darn her sarcasm.

"If we ate doughnuts more than once a week, we'd all be barn-size, Jane."

Yeah, well. Barns were peaceful. They lounged about on golden prairies under blue skies and didn't have to tangle with dangerous, sexy, six-foot-two attitude problems. Barns didn't worry about depressed relatives, cash flow, client referrals or hairy flower arrangements.

"But I didn't get any of the crèmes," she heard herself whine.

Lilia shook her head at her. "Would you like some coffee? I'll bring you some."

"Thanks. Travel mug, please. I have to head to Zantyne today and evaluate that client in the workplace."

"Well, I hope you have better luck there than with that vase of dried flowers. What exactly are you trying to achieve?"

"I'm dusting them," Jane said proudly.

"Mmm."

The tone of Lilia's voice suggested that she check on her project. Jane squinted in disbelief. The fan had taken care of the dust, all right. But it had also blown off all the petals and leaves on the left side of the flowers, leaving the ones on the right intact. They looked partially shaved, and she had a huge mess to clean up off the floor and coffee table.

Jane switched off the fan, turned the bald side of the flowers to the wall and threw the appliance back in the closet. She determined to write a letter to HGTV right away, begging for their advice. There just *had* to be a way to dust dried flowers.

THE CONNECTICUT HEADQUARTERS of Zantyne Pharmaceuticals was a rectangular brown monstrosity that reminded Jane of a monumental loaf of bread. Clearly extra funds were channeled into R & D and not atmosphere.

The inside walls of the place were painted the shade of provolone cheese, and the reception desk was a mossy green. Jane decided she'd stepped into a rather unappetizing corporate sandwich. She asked politely for Dominic.

"Mr. Sayers?" said Zantyne's receptionist into her headset. "Ms. Jane O'Toole to see you." She paused, then nodded. "I'll do that."

Jane wondered if her unwilling client had issued orders to kick her butt right out the door. She unconsciously braced herself for two burly men in security uniforms to appear, but it didn't happen. The sleek blonde got to her feet and said, "Right this way."

Jane followed the pink-clad, entirely too pert

globes of the receptionist's rear end as they twitched through a set of wide double doors and down a taupe-carpeted hallway, until she stopped at an office on the right. Miss Pink flipped her hair over her shoulder and gushed, "Here she is, Dom. Can I get you two anything?"

Oh, maybe a couple of pistols, thought Jane. *Or better yet, lances—so we can run each other through with more gore.*

"Thanks, Jeannie, but I think we're all set." Dom flashed her a surprisingly tusk-free smile as he stood up from his desk, his powerful sex appeal sending much of Jane's blood rushing south.

With a little moue of her lips that made a couple of cute dimples appear, the receptionist wiggled back to her post. Jane was positive Miss Pink had practiced that lip thing in a mirror. Hmm. Maybe she should try it?

Sayers turned the smile upon her now. "Jane!" he said warmly. "Good to see you again. How are you today?"

She stared at him, wary. *Embarrassed that you managed to star naked in my dreams last night.* "Uh, fine," she said. "How are you?"

"Couldn't be better, thanks."

Did someone spray happy mist in your Wheaties this morning? Add amphetamines?

"Would you like something to drink? Coffee?"

She shook her head, unable to look away from a sexy little mole in the middle of his left cheek.

"Tea?"

"No, thank you." *And don't say "me" next, either. Where is your evil twin? The one I met yesterday?*

Today's Dominic was even dressed in a happy-colored pale yellow button-down and khakis, not the funereal pinstripes of the day before. His eyebrows looked less menacing. And dark, curly hairs beckoned to her from his open neckline, cranking up his sex appeal factor even more, if that were possible. *Uh-oh.*

Me, Tarzan, those little curly hairs crooned. *You, Jane. Wanna swing to nirvana on my big, thick vine?*

Huh. She averted her eyes from the danger spot and reminded herself that the man in front of her was nothing more than a chest-thumping primate who needed to be civilized.

She considered asking him to pull his anger out of the nearest file cabinet so they could get on with examining it but decided to go ahead and explore this warm and fuzzy aspect of his personality—since, after all, it was probably a mask. He'd let it slip sooner or later.

"I'm guessing you just want to follow me around and observe me, correct?"

"Yes. I may tape some conversations, too—with your permission."

"Of course!" he said in genial tones.

Who are you?

"To start with, I have a staff meeting in five minutes. You can meet my team and see that I actually play quite well with others."

We'll see about that.

But it was true. Five people filed into the room, including his marketing coordinator, two analysts, an assistant product manager and a PR specialist. Three of them were women, two men. They all seemed to have an easy camaraderie with "Dom," as they called him.

He introduced every person to her by name, joking that Jane was there to help him mind his p's and q's. They all looked puzzled but carried on with various reports to him.

When Jackie, the marketing coordinator, had finished, he thanked her graciously. "And how's Tommy doing?" he asked.

She rolled her eyes. "Kid's gonna drive me crazy, whining about that cast on his arm."

Dom shook his head in sympathy. "Well, tell him he's lucky he didn't break it in the summertime. A cast gets even hotter and itchier then, believe me."

She nodded.

"Your Buccaneers are looking good, Tim." Dom said to one of the analysts.

The guy flashed a big white grin at him. "Yeah. Gonna kick the he—uh, *hoo-ha* outta the Falcons."

"Oh, I wouldn't be too sure about that. Whatcha got for me?"

Tim made his report while Dom nodded thoughtfully.

Jane taped the meeting and took notes with growing incredulity. But they couldn't possibly have all gotten together and rehearsed beforehand. No, these people actually *liked* Sayers. And that didn't add up.

Hmm. She tapped her pen on her nose. And so, clearly, had the company receptionist. But while she'd written that off to a sweet young thing's infatuation with his looks, she couldn't write off the interactions in this meeting. It was all very peculiar. For an instant she wondered if just maybe he'd been telling the truth in her office. That he was being set up by a power-hungry boss.

But no—that was ridiculous. She *knew* Arianna DuBose, was a member of the Kiwanis Club with her and the local women executives' networking group, too. She'd never seen Arianna be anything other than charming, articulate and beautifully dressed. And the woman was in a position of power already—so there was no need for her to backstab or get Machiavellian.

Sayers was an educated white male of a certain age, with certain expectations. And he'd felt anger when a woman was promoted over him—plain and simple. It didn't take her behavioral psych degree to figure that out.

Why, then, did he seem to get along so well with the women in this room? *Oh, lightbulb, Jane. They work for him. Not vice versa. It's easy to be gracious when you've got the power.* Satisfied, she stopped hitting her nose with her pen and capped it, ignoring the quirk of Sayers's lips. *Go ahead and smirk at me, you yutz. You're not stumping me by this charming behavior. I've got you figured out.*

While he took in another report, she allowed herself to assess his looks again from the corner of her eye.

Nice tapered waist. Long thighs. Solid, athletic-looking knees—no skinny knobs visible through the pants. So he probably had good legs, not chicken sticks. She peeked at the chest hair again, which was a bad idea, since it got her wondering about the broad chest underneath.

Jane, get a hold of yourself! You cannot have a fantasy about the man right in front of him.

Aw, but I've got such a good one, her libido whined. *Listen: it involves a furry rug before a roaring fire on a cold, winter night…and he licks melted chocolate and marshmallows off your—*

Stop it! She noticed that she was again tapping on her nose with her pen. She recapped it for the second time. Usually she tapped on the earpiece of her glasses, but she'd been curiously reluctant to put them on in front of Dominic.

He looked over at her and now both corners of his delectable mouth turned up.

Trying to sucker me? Not a chance. She returned his gaze coolly and waited for the meeting to be over, which it soon was. Her stomach growled audibly as he turned to her.

"Care for some lunch?"

Should she go to lunch with him? She hesitated. Well, she could observe him further with other people. Why not? "Okay," she said. "I just need to run to the ladies' room first."

"Good thing," Dominic responded.

Good thing? Why would he possibly care that she took a tinkle? Bizarre man. Jane hitched the strap of her briefcase over her shoulder and marched down the hall to the relevant door. She availed herself of the amenities, still puzzling.

It was when she went to wash her hands that she figured it out. Blue pen marks adorned her nose, making her look like a refugee from the Bic warrior tribe.

She stared at them with growing mortification. How long had they been there? Why hadn't one of the other six people in the room said something? And how was she going to get them off?

Jane dropped her briefcase on the floor and went to town with the pink liquid soap and a brown paper towel, only succeeding in removing all the makeup from the lower half of her face. The pen marks, however, still remained.

She might as well draw a mustache on her lip or add kitty whiskers. No wonder Dominic Sayers had smirked at her!

The score between them was temporarily even, but she'd fix that—and him. There was no doubt in her mind, no doubt at all, about who was going to end up on top….

4

DOMINIC OBSERVED JANE quizzically as they moved their trays through the salad buffet at a local restaurant. The skin on and around her nose seemed extremely…thick. And very…nonshiny. Powdered. But somehow red underneath. His deductive powers told him that she had scrubbed her skin vigorously and then applied almost an entire jar of makeup to the offending area, and he pressed his lips together to keep from laughing. Because underneath it all, he could still detect faint bluish lines.

In spite of them, she was still beautiful, even with that schoolmarm's pout on her pretty lips. He ran an appreciative gaze over her curves, lingering again on her breasts. Damn that jacket. The things ought to be outlawed for women….

Miss Bic squinted, peered and then selected carefully from the salad offerings. No iceberg lettuce. Only red leaf. And only the freshest-looking pieces. Anything with even a suspicion of brown went right back into the large steel lettuce bin. Miss Bic seemed highly irritated by the clear plastic barrier over the salad bar. She peered through it, eyes again squinted, and steamed it up with her breath.

"Forget your glasses?" Dom asked.

"No. How do you know I wear glasses?"

"Oh, just a guess." *Because you've just about flattened your nose against the Plexiglas, there, sweetheart. And if only I'd met you in a different context, I'd love for you to get that close to me.*

She straightened but squinted even more as she wielded the salad tongs over a container of cherry tomatoes and snatched one.

"That one's squishy," Dom told her. *A characteristic to be avoided in tomatoes but sought after in breasts.*

She dropped it and glared at him. "Thank you." She scrunched her eyes and hunched over the clear plastic again, nearsightedly fishing for perfection.

"Would you like me to help you?" Dom asked.

"No, I'm fine."

"That one on the far right, in the corner, is Without Flaw. No green edges, no wrinkles, no dark spots, no puckering."

She deliberately took a different one, and Dom shook his head. Exactly four others joined their buddy on her plate.

Miss Bic bypassed the next container completely—no fatty pepperoni for her—but picked precisely five quarters of marinated artichoke from the next bin. And then five slices of cucumber, followed by five slices of red pepper, which, he supposed, color-coordinated with the five cherry tomatoes. For protein she chose small slices of grilled chicken: five.

What was with the magic number? Dom was almost disappointed when Jane used only one ladleful of fat-free Italian dressing.

He took his own tray and followed her back to their table, unloading his heaping bowl of chili and massive iceberg lettuce salad under her gaze.

Her eyes widened as he added a few shakes of hot sauce to the chili, and he grinned. "Don't worry—I used exactly five shakes."

Spots of pink appeared in Jane's cheeks and spread to her ears, which he could see now since she'd stuffed her hair behind them. They were very cute ears. He'd really like to lick one—just taste it.

"So what's with the number five?" Dom asked.

Jane shrugged. "I don't know. I just like it."

"It's a nice, clean number," Dom mused. "Half of ten."

Jane started to look annoyed.

"No extra digits to mess it up. No ambiguity about it. It's reasonable. Not too high, not too low. Right in the middle."

"I thought I was supposed to be analyzing *your* behavior," Jane said.

"Turnabout's fair play." He spooned chili into his mouth and tried not to stare at the blue lines still visible to the right of her nose.

She touched the area self-consciously. "I don't know what it says about me, but the number five has always been my favorite. We have five fingers on each hand. Five toes on each foot. We have two arms, two legs and a head. If you connect those five points in a continuum, you make a circle."

"Da Vinci," he said.

"Exactly."

He waited.

She fidgeted. "And…oh, I don't know. Five times five is twenty-five, which is point two five of a hundred, one clean quarter…" She gave a self-conscious laugh. "You probably think I'm a crazy woman."

"No." Dom held his spoon wrong side up, the curve of it against his bottom lip. "I think you're a very precise, analytical woman. You draw logical conclusions. You're no fuss, no muss and you make decisions based on orderly sets of facts."

Jane stared at him. "And how else are you supposed to make decisions? Isn't that the right way?"

"Aha," Dom said. "So according to you, there's a right way and a wrong way to make a decision, then."

Jane stabbed a piece of red pepper and stuck it in her mouth. Simultaneously she took a deep, deliberately calm breath. Both multitasking and playing for time, Dom thought. Efficient. Intelligent. Rigid.

And dangerous to him. He'd already given her too much ammunition to draw conclusions about him—especially if she was a rigid personality. He hoped this morning's meeting had shown her that he wasn't as much of a jerk as he'd appeared to be in her office.

But maybe she'd decided that it was all a dog and pony show for her benefit. Or worse, that he was some kind of split personality. Oh, great…he could just see himself explaining to her. "Oh, that guy you met at first? That was Dirk, my mean side. But he only pops out every once in a while. Dominic, the nice guy? He's around the majority of the time. He's the one you want to evaluate, not Dirk." *And then there's Drew, the horny goat-man who'd like to back you up against a wall and…*

Uh-huh. Was it better to have Miss Bic think he was a pig or just a garden-variety psycho? Dom spooned some more chili into his mouth and wondered how he'd arrived at this point in his life. He also wondered how he was going to convince Miss Bic that Arianna was the split-personality psycho, not him.

JANE CRUNCHED DOWN ON HER vegetables and pondered the corner into which Dominic Sayers was trying to back her.

If she admitted that yes, she did feel that there was a right way versus a wrong way to make a decision, then his next step would be to show her that she had drawn erroneous conclusions about him, based upon skewed logic. And really, any logic could be turned upon its ear if you messed around with it long enough…because logic was based on assumptions. *Aaaarrrrgggghhhh!*

Jane decided right then that she strongly disliked Dominic Sayers. Because of him, she had drawn blue marks around her nose. Because of him, she had not put on her glasses, and still refused to put them on, even though she needed them to see and they were in the side pocket of her purse. And because of him, she hadn't slept much last night and was now questioning her ways of thinking.

Because of Dominic Sayers, she was being silly, vain and illogical. And she was none of these things on a normal day under normal circumstances. The abnormality was *him*, Dominic Sayers. There was nothing wrong with her. *He* was the one who needed help.

Jane, now firmly back on the comfortable cushion of her superiority, refrained from slapping herself in the forehead. Of course Sayers was trying to force her to question herself. He wanted to challenge all of her assumptions about him. He wanted to con her into thinking he was the very model of a modern management man.

Which he isn't. He obviously had issues about answering to women, and she was, after all, a woman. To whom he had to answer. *So he wants to get my panties in a wad. And he's made a good start, darn it.*

Jane took another bite of her salad and aimed a pleasant smile at Dom. "How's your chili?"

"Full of beans." He looked at her with a bland expression.

Jane narrowed her eyes, but he gazed back without a blink. *Full of beans, huh? He's referring to my profession, and not his food.* But she let it pass.

"Dominic," she asked, "why did you invite me to lunch?"

"It was the polite thing to do," he said with a quirk of his lips. "And I'm a polite guy."

"You weren't polite the last time we met."

"True. But I hadn't planned on being stuck with you then."

Her mouth opened in surprise at his candor, and without planning to, she laughed. "But since you're stuck with me now…?"

"I might as well charm you. After all—" he smiled winningly "—charming you is in my best interests, you will agree."

Again her mouth opened. This time she covered it with her hand to smother the laugh. *He's incorrigible.*

"Oh, don't do that." Dominic grasped her fingers in his large paw—*zing!*—and pulled them down to the table. "You have a beautiful smile. Don't hide it."

Where had the zing come from? Being touched inappropriately by a grizzly bear should not produce a zing, darn it. Jane reclaimed her hand from under his paw and wrapped her fingers around her fork, wielding the utensil like a weapon.

She stabbed a piece of grilled chicken and waved it at him. "Do you really think I'm that easy to manipulate?"

"Oh, no—don't assume that I've underestimated you. I think you'll be a real chore to manipulate." His eyes danced.

She gaped at him again. How did he think he could

get away with saying such things? Part of her was offended. Yet part of her admired his honesty—even though it bordered on the obnoxious.

"Listen, Sayers." Though she couldn't help but respond to the twinkle in his eyes, she kept her tone firm. "You cannot charm me into a positive evaluation. I'm a professional, not an eighteen-year-old coed. And I'm not looking at how you interact with *me*. I'm observing your behavior in the workplace."

He nodded. "Understood. So I'm only exercising my charm around you to stay in practice." Sayers dug back into his chili while she stared at him, fighting the desire to bang her forehead on the table.

He leaned the underside of his spoon against his lower lip again, gently tapping, and she saw her face reflected in it upside down, contorting like taffy and looking utterly ridiculous.

The fingers grasping the spoon dwarfed it, but Sayers's hand wasn't really like a paw at all. It possessed an unexpected elegance, a teasing masculinity that crept somehow under her skin and set her nerves aflame.

Damn it, damn it, damn it, thought Jane. *I refuse to envy a spoon. I refuse!*

But those fingers of Dom's, the zing fingers, wrapped all the way around the stainless steel, caressing it. Leaving faint whorls printed on the metal.

She wondered what his fingertips would feel like on her skin, and an unbidden image of them stroking down her spine produced a delicious shiver.

Which of course he noticed. Dom quirked an eyebrow at her. "Cold?" he asked, lips still against the bowl of the spoon.

She shook her head, instructing herself to look away from his mouth. How curious that she'd never really examined the human mouth…the web of tiny lines and miraculous tissues and curious curves that created a lip. Two lips. What had inspired God to create the human lip?

Eat. Your. Salad. Logic and professionalism said it to her. *You. Brainless. Bimbo.* Lips, for God's sake! If she didn't snap out of this, she might as well pull her own upper lip all the way over her head and go home.

Jane forked up a slice of cucumber and waved it through the air at Dom. *Say something, idiot!* But she landed it back in her bowl like a little UFO on a practice run.

"Let me guess," prompted Dom. "That piece of cucumber has more than five seeds, which renders it unacceptable."

"Huh?"

He was openly laughing at her now. "Or is it a little too green? At least eat your chicken, Jane. You need protein to sustain this level of neurosis."

She tossed her napkin on the table and glared at him. "Sayers, you're presuming a familiarity between us which does not exist and *will* not exist. I'll give you the benefit of the doubt and assume that you're attempting to tease me and not outright insult me, but we need to get that clear. I am not neurotic. I just happen to like fresh vegetables, okay?"

"I stand corrected and chastened, Jane." He looked anything but. "And I would never dare to get familiar with you. Unless of course you wanted me to." He grinned.

His words sent a flash of heat through her and she shifted in her seat uncomfortably. She didn't dare acknowledge it, but the heat grew as she pictured Dominic getting familiar with her…right under the restaurant table…with a bare foot, his fingers or, even more shocking, his tongue?

She almost gasped out loud at the image and she knew she needed to recover now, immediately, or he would read her thoughts; sense her state of arousal.

"Is this how you behave around Arianna DuBose?"

Dominic's eyes flashed. His nostrils flared. His lips flattened into a thin line. His jaw tightened. "No."

He picked up the check and fished his wallet out of a back pocket, then slapped the bill down with a credit card.

"You're not paying for my lunch," Jane said evenly.

"I am."

She pulled her purse onto her lap and dug out her wallet, catching the corner of her glasses with the flap. They clattered onto the tabletop and she felt herself flush dark red.

Ignoring them and avoiding his sardonic gaze, she pulled a twenty out of her wallet and placed it on top of his credit card.

"We'll go Dutch. I don't want any questions raised about the objectivity of my evaluation."

He stood up. "Did I understand correctly? That must mean you haven't already made up your mind." His voice dripped sarcasm.

Pig. Jane stood up, too. Then she jammed her glasses onto her nose and marched out of the restaurant ahead of him.

5

JANE SAT WITH HER ARMS FOLDED and stared straight ahead during the ride back to Zantyne Pharmaceuticals.

"You must be seeing things much more clearly now." Dominic's sarcasm had not abated.

"Yes, I am. How funny that I'd forgotten my glasses were right in my purse the entire time."

She wasn't fooling him and they both knew it. He smirked with the knowledge that she'd wanted to be attractive for him and not look schoolmarmish.

She wanted to mug him of that realization and smack the smirk into next year. *Pig.*

Silently she recanted the insult, remembering that she was supposed to be a professional, and professionals remained objective in situations like this. *I neither like nor dislike Dominic wanking Sayers.* Ahem.

Try again, Jane. *I neither like nor dislike Dominic Sayers. I neither li—*

"Front-door service with a smile," he interrupted her affirmations. "It's wet, nasty weather, so I'll let you out here and go park the car on my own."

Jane blinked. "Thank you," she said, getting out of his car. She had to admit that pigs weren't generally gentlemen. *I neither like nor dislike Dominic Sayers....*

DOMINIC WATCHED JANE O'TOOLE as she walked crisply in her London Fog to the doors of Zantyne and pulled one open with a little more force than necessary. Every hair on her head seemed to quiver with indignation, and her glasses glinted with it, too.

Well, doesn't the truth hurt, sweetheart. You had *made up your mind about me and you don't like being called on it.*

Dom snorted. "Objectivity, my ass." He pulled the Jaguar into a parking slot and sat there for a moment, reflecting about his situation. He wasn't sure why one moment he liked Jane O'Toole and the next he despised her. He also wasn't sure why he was charming to her one moment and then insulting the next. And if there was one thing he hated, it was not being sure. Dominic had built a career on his confidence. And it was genuine—because he knew he was good. He wasn't simply a cocky poseur; he was the real thing.

Right now it didn't matter if he was good or confident, however. He was being knocked off balance by a woman who didn't play according to any rule book or ethical standard familiar to him. Arianna made up her own version of morality, and Jane was her puppet.

Dom drummed his fingertips on the taupe leather seat. If he didn't figure out how to beat these women at their own game, that leather seat wouldn't belong to him for long. He'd be fired and lucky to be behind the wheel of a hot-dog cart.

He got out of the Jag and stood in the rain, pondering the situation from every angle. The image of Jane's mortified face as she'd settled her glasses onto her nose brought a smile to his face.

There was no doubt in his mind that she was as attracted to him as he was to her. And if that was her Achilles' heel, well, then…he intended to nibble on it. Among other things.

See Jane squirm. See Jane moan. See Jane beg.

If those two women could play dirty, then so, by God, could he. Dom tossed his keys in the air, palmed them again and hit the Jaguar's lock button by feel. Then, with a tuneless whistle, he sauntered across the parking lot and inside.

ARIANNA DUBOSE WAVED AT JANE as she walked by her open door. She held up a finger, as she was on the phone, but motioned Jane to come in and sit down opposite her desk.

As she waited for the female vice president to finish the call, Jane took stock of her one more time. She'd met Arianna a few times at business functions. She'd spoken at the local Kiwanis Club, and they'd sat next to each other at the last Executive Women in Business luncheon. She vaguely remembered that Arianna ate nothing, absolutely nothing, but meat.

Arianna was exceptionally well groomed and studded with diamonds at her ears, fingers and neck. Each rock was at least a carat of success and brilliance. She sported a platinum wristwatch, blood-red nails and lips and black helmet hair.

Jane caught a glimpse of black lace under the woman's business blouse—interesting—and told herself not to be bitchy when she noticed that the VP's bustline seemed unnaturally firm and unforgiving. If Arianna had been surgically enhanced, it was none of her business.

Jane didn't deliberately listen to Arianna's conversation, but she couldn't help picking up a few tidbits.

"No, Harold, that's not acceptable. Absolutely not. I don't care what the excuses are—you're meeting that November deadline, whether IT comes through or not. If you have to go door-to-door and fill out the surveys by hand, then so be it."

"Harold. Harold, don't even think about threatening me. You quit now, I'll make sure you never work in pharmaceuticals again. Got it? Good." Arianna hung up the phone with a snarl but immediately downshifted it into a warm purr for Jane's benefit.

"Jane!" She surged from behind her desk and grasped both of Jane's hands in her cold, dry ones. "How are you?"

"Fine, thanks. How are you?"

Arianna waved in irritation at the phone. "Oh, just working out a few kinks with marketing on a new product. These guys are like a bunch of slow toddlers, for God's sake! I can't keep wiping their noses for them. They know what the market demands and they know what it takes to keep our competitive edge. I don't want to hear their pathetic whining about how they can't make deadlines."

Jane nodded in sympathy.

"Men fall into two categories," Arianna expounded, "toddlers or teenagers. The toddlers whine and cry and are generally incompetent, and the teenagers just give you lip and attitude. Dominic Sayers, for example, is a teenager."

"Oh?"

"My God, yes. And I simply won't put up with his insubordination." She cast a glance into the hallway and shut her door. "So what have your impressions been so far?"

"Well," said Jane carefully, "he definitely seems to be a strong personality."

Arianna laughed. "Honey, you don't have to be tactful around me. He's an *asshole*. And he believes he's a lot smarter than he really is. And he thinks with his pecker. He just can't handle having a woman in charge."

"Mmm," said Jane, trying not to think about Dominic's pecker. "Well, in order to do a full evaluation, I need to observe quite a bit more and do some experimentation with role-playing. Have him take some tests. That sort of thing."

Arianna blinked impatiently and pulled a nail file from her top desk drawer. Using precise slicing movements in one direction only, she smoothed the edge of each nail on her left hand. "How long—" slice, slice "—is all of this going to take?"

Jane knit her brows as she gazed at the woman. "Well, at least a few weeks. Why? Are you on a time-line of some kind?"

Arianna transferred the nail file to the other hand and went to work. "Not at all," she said just a shade too casually. "I just like to know about these things up front."

Jane nodded.

"By the way," Arianna began, changing the subject. "Have I mentioned that I'd like to see you work with HR at Zantyne on a national level? To orchestrate some company-wide seminars like Breaking New Ground and Morale Boosting?"

"No, you didn't mention that," said Jane, her pulse quickening. "But I'd love to!" What a coup for a new company like Finesse! They would definitely break even, maybe even make a profit in their first year, with just *one* such client. Jane tried not to salivate openly.

"Let's talk about a presentation, then," Arianna nodded. "Of course you'll have my full backing…assuming that I'm pleased with the way you handle this current issue." She laughed a too-melodious laugh. "And I'm sure I will be."

Jane nodded and smiled. "Of course. Finesse may be a fledgling company, but we're aptly named and very professional."

"I can see that, Jane. I'm sure this is the beginning of a long and profitable relationship for us both." Arianna smiled broadly.

My goodness, her teeth are white. Almost blinding. Jane followed Arianna to her office door and shook her hand as the vice president showed her out. Did the woman gargle with Clorox?

HER DAD AND GILBEY WEREN'T too talkative at this Sunday dinner, either, even though Jane brought Lilia. Lil brought a beautifully wrapped bouquet of mixed flowers and wore a sapphire-blue silk blouse for the occasion.

Jane shook her head and grinned. "Miss Manners, honey, this is my dad and the backyard grill, not dinner at the White House."

Her friend raised a brow. "So? Even a picnic table can use some fresh blooms. And I'm not going to show up empty-handed."

Jane gave her a fond glance and let her be but had to laugh when her dad just stared at the flowers and then back at Lilia.

"What, nobody's ever brought you flowers before?"

"Uh, thanks, hon."

"Dad, you might want to put them in a vase. Or a pitcher. I know we have a pitcher around here somewhere."

"Right." Her father ambled into the kitchen and poked around in a few of the blue-painted cabinets, coming up empty-handed. Finally he opened the refrigerator and grabbed a plastic container with a swallow of orange juice left in it, which he poured down the sink. He rinsed the thing, refilled it with water and plunked the blossoms into it with a small grunt of satisfaction.

Lilia kissed him on the cheek. "They look lovely. Shall I put them on the picnic table outside?"

He nodded, and Lil followed Jane out the back door. Gilbey was headed in their direction from the barn on the back of the property. They waved and he waved back.

"Your dad's as talkative as ever," Lil murmured.

Jane laughed. "He'll never change. But we love him just the way he is." It was Gilbey she worried about. Her dad was close to retiring from the tool-and-die shop he managed. Gil had the rest of his life ahead of him. She wanted to see him productive and happy.

"Hi, Lil. Hey, Jane," he greeted them. "What's up?"

The conversation didn't get much more sparkling than that, as they all sat at the weathered old picnic table under the elms and consumed their burgers in the cool October air.

Lil, ever good-mannered and good-natured, tried valiantly to keep the conversation flowing, but Emily Post herself would have been stymied.

Jane's dad answered in monosyllables, and Gilbey began to draw Lilia on his napkin. He really was talented artistically.

"Hey, Gil," Jane said to him. "That's wonderful!" He'd perfectly captured Lil's high cheekbones, dark winged brows and the curve of her mouth.

Lilia nodded. "You're very good."

"Gilbey, have you thought about working for an

advertising agency? Do you want me to help you put together a portfolio?" Jane tried to nudge him as gently as possible.

Her brother sighed and laid down his pencil. "Jane, I've had it with meaningless jobs and other people's orders and their silly products. I can't be a cog in the wheel. I know you do this out of love, but I wish you'd leave me alone."

"I'm sorry," she said, stung. "I'm just trying to help."

"Well, quit." He dropped his burger and ran a hand through his longish hair. "You wanna know what I love? What I want to spend my life doing?" He pushed back abruptly from the table. "Follow me."

All three of them trailed after Gil to the old barn. He threw open the door and gestured for them to look.

A dozen strange but lovely structures met their eyes. Created out of brightly painted scrap metal and "found" objects, Gilbey's creations were both abstract and animated, half mechanical, half animal. They were full of personality.

He'd used automobile and bicycle and lawnmower parts, welding them together in odd juxtapositions and incongruous patterns.

Jane had never seen anything like them before. She wasn't sure what they were. But she loved them. So, from the look on her face, did Lilia.

Only her dad rubbed the back of his neck and asked, "What the hell you been smokin' out here, boy?"

"Dad!" Jane shot him a warning glance. "They're fantastic. Gil, these should be in a modern gallery."

Her brother shrugged.

"I'm serious!"

"Gil, she's right," said Lil.

Jane turned to her, snapping her fingers. "What's the name of that guy? The friend of yours who's a professional photographer?"

"Jim."

"Yeah, him. Let's get him out here to take some slides—"

"Jane," said Gilbey.

"—and we'll make a list of galleries to send—" she stopped, looking at Gilbey's expression.

"You're doing it again." He folded his arms.

"What?"

"Trying to manage my life."

"But—"

Lilia laid a hand on her arm.

Jane sighed. "Sorry. But can we at least put you in touch with Jim? Will you let him take the slides? Gil, this work is too good to be hidden away in a Connecticut barn."

"I'll think about it," her brother said.

And she had to be satisfied with that.

ON MONDAY, JANE WALKED THROUGH the front door of Finesse and hung up her raincoat. She stared blankly at the hairy dried rose halves and tried to focus on whatever it was that was bothering her.

That brief meeting with Arianna DuBose last week? Dom's sarcasm?

Unconsciously she reached for a pen on her desk and began spinning it between her fingers.

Dominic Sayers's face wouldn't get out of her head—his expression sardonic, blasé and…disappointed.

Disappointed? Yes. She had definitely seen a puzzling disappointment. In *her*. In the world at large. As if some ideal of Dominic's had been tarnished.

But the concept of an idealistic Dominic didn't fit with her image of a cutthroat man on the make furious that a woman had gotten in the way of his ambition.

For surely a man with ideals that could be disappointed was a man who was vulnerable. And Sayers didn't seem vulnerable in any way, shape or form.

Something else was niggling at her. Whereas she should be ecstatic about the possibility of a fat corporate contract with Zantyne, backed by Arianna, she felt uncomfortable with the idea instead.

Arianna had been so smooth. So…smug, almost. So sure of Jane's reaction to the offer and her instinctive response of gratitude. Arianna was playing her. She felt like an unwary insect that had just landed on the tongue of a Venus flytrap.

But that was ridiculous. She'd seen male hostility in this type of situation before. It was nothing new. And she'd seen her own brother blame countless bosses for his problems at work. Nobody liked to take responsibility for their part in a difficult relationship. *Human nature is firmly planted in self-interest and often blind to personal failings.*

Shannon strolled to Jane's office door and stuck her head in. "Hiya. So how'd it go the other day?"

Jane realized that she was now tapping on her nose with the pen. She tossed it down. Hadn't she learned? "Hey, Shan. It went okay. Actually you could say it went really well." So why couldn't *she* say that? "I talked with that female VP, the DuBose woman, and she'd like to see a presentation from us on some employee development training seminars. For the entire company—and it's big. International."

"Fabulous! I smell actual salaries in the air if we get a contract like that." Shannon threw her arms into the air and spun around on one foot.

"You know," Jane told her, "if I did that, I'd look like a possessed flamingo. But you make it look hip."

"That's 'cause I am so hip, it hurts." Shannon shimmied her pelvis while managing to snake her bust around, too.

"What are you, part python?"

Shannon stopped and peered at her. "What the *hell* is that on your face, sweet cheeks? You got varicose veins on your nose?"

Jane ducked her head and muttered, "Go away."

Shannon plucked the pen from Jane's blotter and examined the color. "Honey, you want to draw on your face, think Aveda, Trish McEvoy, even Cover Girl! Not Bic. And blue is definitely not your color."

"I thought it was kinda retro chic," Jane joked.

"No. No, no, no, and I repeat, no. Not on you."

"We cannot all be goddesses of style, okay?"

Shannon sidled one of her perfect buns onto Jane's desk and leaned her weight on it. "There's nothing wrong with your style, Jane. I'm just teasing you— and, of course, suggesting that you use pencils for a while, until you break this nervous habit of scribbling on your face."

"I've got a lot of habits I need to break," muttered Jane. "But I'm better at helping other people break theirs."

"Oh, I hear you. Now what's bothering you? Your appearance, the fact that Sayers is hot or the horrible news that we might make tons of money off Zantyne?"

"What's bothering me," said Jane slowly, "is my instincts. This Sayers guy is difficult, no doubt. But he's sort of an honest difficult, if you know what I mean."

"Okaaaay." Shannon pursed her lips.

"And there's something a little off about the VP— the one hinting about all the business she can give us. I don't like it…and I'm not sure I like her."

"But you don't seem to like him, either."

Jane hesitated. "True."

"And it's not a requirement that we like all the clients we work with. It's a little unrealistic to expect to adore every person we deal with professionally."

"Yeah, I know. You're right."

"So just do the job, fill out the evaluation on him. After all, you're not being asked to evaluate *her*. She's beside the point."

"Not totally. Since she's sort of offering a bribe if she gets the results she wants from me."

Shannon scooted off the desk and walked to the window, folding her arms across her chest. "Janey, I hate to say it, but that's the way the world works. You scratch her back, she'll scratch yours." She let out a hard, cynical laugh. "That's the way the entire city of L.A. operates."

Jane frowned. "God, you're so jaded."

Shannon spun on her heel and stared her down. "I have reason to be, and you know it."

"Well, first, this is not L.A., it's New England, hub of plainspoken Yankees. Second, I refuse to compromise my integrity—"

"Whoa, Jane. Step carefully, okay?"

Jane looked down at her hands, picked at her short, practical nails. "Shan, I'm sorry. I didn't mean it that way. And we both know that you didn't sleep with that director just to get the role. You were in love with the guy."

"Was I? Or did I just convince myself of that because it was convenient? I'm not sure any longer, Jane. That's how bad L.A. can screw you up. That's why I left. I didn't even know who I was anymore."

Shannon hunched her shoulders and blew out a breath while Jane observed her in silence. Shan had returned from California after six years of trying to make it as an actress. She'd come back a different woman, sad and burned out.

Jane stood up and hugged Shannon, refused to let go even when she stood there, rigid, not hugging back. It was classic body language: Shan didn't feel she deserved the hug, didn't feel worthy of it, couldn't accept it.

"Listen to me, you stubborn wench," Jane said. "I don't believe that for a second. And if you'll stop flogging yourself for one moment, you won't believe it, either. Even if you were tempted, you had the moxie to walk away from the role once you found out about him. So stop tormenting yourself and pretending that you have no heart. I know better."

"Huh." But Shannon actually leaned into her for a moment, patted her back before pulling away.

Jane knew it was a very small step but a step nonetheless. And she would help Shannon take others. Because her friend was far too beautiful and talented and loving to have such low self-esteem. The only thing she was right about was that L.A. had screwed her up.

"Shannon, it's L.A. that has no heart, not you. You're amazing and creative and you have a sense of style most women would kill for."

"Stop it, you're embarrassing me."

"Well, it's true, sweetie. And you're packing in executive clients who pay you to dress them and make them over. You're in demand." Jane checked her watch. "I've got to go—I have a client, Mrs. Collins, coming now."

"Okay." Shannon got halfway to her office before turning around. "Hey, Jane?"

"Mmm?"

"Thanks."

THAT JANE'S CLIENT, LISA Collins, had no self-esteem was an understatement. Shoulders bowed, head down, she shuffled into the office and waited to be asked before sitting down. "Thanks for seeing me," she mumbled.

"Of course. How can I help you?"

"Well, it's my, um, boss. She acts as if she's the queen of the universe and I'm her slave."

"I see. Well, let me ask the most obvious question first. Have you thought about changing jobs?"

Lisa crossed her legs, then tugged at her skirt. Then she uncrossed and recrossed them. "Well, yeah. I've done that three times now. But this situation keeps happening. It's like I have a Kick Me sign on my back. I'm a good employee, I do exactly what I'm told, I'm never late, I work extra without complaining. I don't know why I get treated so poorly. Like I have no life of my own and have nothing better to do than serve. And *now* she wants me to work through the vacation I've had planned for a year!"

Jane made a sympathetic noise. "Have you tried saying no?"

Lisa swallowed. "I'm afraid I'll get fired."

Jane leaned forward. "But, Lisa, you've found three jobs—easily, right?"

The girl nodded.

"So you've found yourself positions with no problem. If for some reason you *did* get fired, would it really be the end of the world?"

Lisa looked shocked. "But I'd get a bad reference!"

"You've got other ones, right? You wouldn't even have to use her. Besides, are you so sure your boss is that unreasonable?"

Lisa hesitated, then shook her head. "I think she just forgot about me being gone for those two weeks."

"And when you reminded her?"

"She got irritated and said she really needed me then. She's preparing for a big sales pitch. But I have plane tickets! And cruise tickets. And a friend's going with me—it'll ruin her vacation, too, if I don't go."

"Okay. You're going to have to stand up for yourself," Jane said.

"I was afraid you were going to say that. How?"

"I'd suggest that you tell her firmly that you have long-standing plans. If she still resists or tries to make you feel guilty, then offer to call a temporary agency to get her some help while you're away. Do not give in."

Lisa still looked uncertain.

"You're assuming you have no power in this situation, and you do," Jane told her.

"I do?"

"Yes. Good, hardworking, intelligent assistants are hard to find these days. You're a precious resource, not a slave."

"I never thought about it that way," said the girl.

Jane nodded. "That's why she has all the power. She doesn't want to fire you, Lisa. She'd have to interview, decide on and train someone else. Most people dislike change."

"You're right...."

"I think you'd benefit from the assertiveness seminar I teach," Jane said. "It's inexpensive and will teach you how to communicate your needs and not get pushed around. Are you interested?"

"You bet," said Lisa. "I'll sign up today."

JANE'S NEXT APPOINTMENT WAS with a middle-aged man named Barry Stall who wanted to take radical steps to improve his health but kept sabotaging himself.

The problem, she explained, was he tried to tackle too much at once. He couldn't quit smoking, lose forty pounds and become a triathlete in one day.

"It takes twenty-one days—and some studies say sixty—to make or break a habit, Barry. I'd advise cutting out the cigarettes first, maybe with a prescription to help you with the cravings." She advised very small, realistic goals.

She also asked him to look at some of the underlying reasons in his life that caused him to treat his body so badly. By the time Barry left, he was feeling a lot more optimistic and had scheduled several more sessions.

Jane was glad they'd connected so well. Now if only *she* could go twenty-one days without eating a doughnut.... On that thought she left her office for the day and found Shannon again.

"Hey, where's Lilia? I think it's time for happy hour."

Shannon looked at her watch and shrugged. "It's after six. I'm game."

"Good." Jane walked to her office door and craned her head out. "Lilia! Hey, Lilia. Drop the Miss Manners book, grab your Chanel bag and loan us some class. It's cosmopolitan time, dahling."

"It's only six-fifteen!" called Lil in her lovely cultured voice. "I'm researching Japanese wedding customs for a client."

Shannon strode to the door. "It's after midnight in London, doll, and we all need a break. Let's go."

"She's waiting for an engraved invitation," Jane teased.

"All right, all right…" Lilia appeared, coat in one hand and lipstick in the other. She applied it elegantly in the gilt-framed mirror by the door. "My hair's a mess."

"Tousled is in, Lil. Let's motor!"

6

JANE WOKE THE NEXT MORNING feeling anything but cosmopolitan. *Ugh.* How had the drink gotten its name? Most likely because a cosmopolitan hangover felt as if an entire city block had collapsed on your head. Along with a few taxis and buses.

She had vague memories of a group of four sales guys sending a round of drinks to their table. Yep, the Ford sales reps, in town for some conference.

Then the group of attorneys had followed suit, not to be bested.

Jane yawned. It was often very inexpensive to go out with Shannon—her voluptuous-blond-goddess stature inspired the most amazing generosity in the opposite sex. They had even gotten a plate of hors d'oeuvres on the house…both a compliment and a smart marketing move. If Shannon frequented the place, so would herds of men.

It would be so easy to hate Shannon, but Jane knew that the attention actually embarrassed and annoyed her. Short of gaining fifty pounds and shaving her head, however, there wasn't much she could do about it—if she wanted to have a life of any kind.

Jane got gingerly out of bed and staggered into the bathroom. Role-playing. She had to freakin' role play with Dominic freakin' Sayers today. This involved cute little "scripts" that they would act out with each other, with her reading the part of the difficult person that Dom had to "manage." Then she'd essentially grade him on how he dealt with the situation. Hidden in the stack were three different scenarios that challenged how he worked with women.

Jane buzzed with a peculiar combination of anticipation and dread at seeing him again.

She should analyze that and get to the bottom of her feelings, but right now she would much rather analyze a s'more-flavored Pop-Tart and some hot coffee.

The s'mores Pop-Tarts were the legacy of her last boyfriend, Pete. Nice guy, Pete. Nothing wrong with him, except for his never-ending fascination for World War II movies and basketball. And the fact that he ate nothing but boxed or canned food.

There was nothing wrong with Pete, nothing at all. But there was nothing particularly right about him, either. Except his taste in Pop-Tarts, which she could buy on her own. Pete was no doubt watching his Flying Aces specials in some other woman's living room now—and stinking up *her* apartment with canned ravioli.

After starting the coffee, Jane hopped into the shower and mentally sidestepped the question of what Dominic Sayers might watch on TV.

"WWE WRESTLING, of course. And The Man Show. Spike TV." Dom leaned back in his black leather chair and shot a look of amusement at Jane O'Toole, who was unresplendent in beige today but still somehow sexy. "Is that part of your psychological profile or just vulgar curiosity?"

Jane's lips tightened. "What gives you the idea that I'd be curious about you?"

"Your choice of major in college and your chosen profession, Jane. You're all about curiosity. You like to analyze what makes people tick. Oh—and the fact that you're not wearing your glasses again today."

Jane pointedly ignored his last comment. "What makes you tick?"

"Now why would I make things so easy for you as to tell you?"

"Because you'd have a better chance of showing me your side of the situation here at Zantyne."

"No." He folded his arms across his chest and stared at her without blinking. "You don't take anything at face value. I told you exactly what was going on at our first meeting, but you chose not to believe me."

Jane threw up her hands. "I have been told two very different versions of what is going on. The truth probably lies somewhere in the middle. Do you expect me not to analyze the situation? How can I evaluate it— or your personality—if I don't gather the facts?"

"Well, as long as it's just the facts, ma'am," he said. He allowed his gaze to roam over her—the neat beige pantsuit buttoned over a small waist and wonderfully womanly hips. He suspected that Jane O'Toole had a figure like a young Marilyn Monroe. But this gentleman didn't prefer blondes. No, he liked Jane's dusky, messy curls. And he especially liked her lush, properly pale pink mouth. He wondered what shade that delicious bottom lip would turn if he…bit it. Sucked on it, long and hard and possessively.

Uh-oh. Jane had been talking—words had issued from between those lips he'd been fantasizing about. Words in his own language, that he should have heard and understood. "Excuse me? I didn't catch what you said."

"I repeat, then. I'd like to do some role-playing with you now."

"Role-playing?" It sounded highly suspicious, not to mention silly.

"Yes. I have with me a series of scripts. I'll tell you who I am in each scenario and read my lines. You respond as you would if the vignette were a real business situation. Okay?"

Dom sighed and nodded. Just how much of his time was she going to waste today?

"By the way, I don't actually watch any of those shows I mentioned. What I do watch includes network news, a couple of true-crime shows and the odd sitcom."

She nodded, made a couple of notes, then looked up and smiled. "I really couldn't picture you being a WWE fan."

"Thank you," he said. "Okay. Let's get on with the role-playing." Actually, the more he thought about it, interesting possibilities popped into his head. For example, Jane could play the part of a skimpily clad French maid, imaginative and clever with a feather duster.

He'd be her demanding employer, the guy who forced her to bend over a lot. Hmm. Yep, he envisioned her in a very short, flouncy black skirt, tiny blouse and starched frilly apron. It tied provocatively in a bow above her bottom. And what better to clean house in than skyscraper heels and black fishnets?

On the other hand, Jane would make a most excellent schoolteacher, and when he was bad—quite often—could take down his pants to, uh, discipline him, the errant student. For that particular role, he saw her in glasses, hair piled on her head, clad in a doll-size sweater and a straight but still only barely decent skirt. Long enough to cover her cheeks, but short enough that they were immediately accessible. Oh, and this skirt should roll up like a window shade at a moment's notice.

This incarnation of Jane really called for sensible shoes, but Dom had never been a big fan of those. So he banished them and fit her with appropriate fantasy wear: CFM pumps and the sheerest of thigh-highs.

Jane might also make a good nurse, one who forced him to take *all* of his clothes off and then pushed him down on an examination table to give him a thorough checkup. Oh, yeah…in this role, she wore a white garter belt and stockings, one of those cute old-fashioned hats and only scraps of other things. *Yeah, baby, grip me there and tell me to turn my head and cough!*

"Sayers!"

"Huh?" Oh, shit. He'd missed whatever it was that she was actually saying again.

"Sayers, are you listening to me?"

"Oh, you had my full attention."

She raised a brow.

"Really."

"All right, then. In this scenario, I am a difficult employee who has barely met, and certainly not exceeded, expectations on the job. I am asking for a raise and a promotion. How do you handle the situation?"

He rolled his eyes. "I say that I will certainly consider you for the job and that you're a good candidate. Then I might mention that the pool of applicants for the position is very competitive and that a certain skill set is necessary to do the job. I ask if you feel you're strong in that area."

"I feel that I'm exceptionally strong in that area. I feel that I'm being underutilized in my current position and definitely underpaid."

Oh, honey, I sure could utilize you. Dom forced himself back on track. "Then, if I want to keep you around, difficult employee, I stroke you and ask you to be patient and point out ways in which you can improve and impress the management team."

Jane waited.

"And if I don't want you to stay, then I bluntly indicate that there are several aspects of your performance that need to be improved."

Jane looked at her notes. "Suppose I don't take that well and create a scene in your office. I begin to cry and carry on."

"I reply that all comments are meant to be constructive and should in no way be construed as personal attacks. I call Human Resources to step in."

Jane nodded. "Okay. Let's look at another scenario."

Okay, sure. You could be my waitress at some gin joint. You're dressed in one of those Minnie Mouse-does-Dallas cocktail getups and you lean far, far forward to take my drink order. I become lost in the mountainous terrain of your womanliness....

Dom burst out laughing, partly because his brain had sent the last words to him in a hideous parody of a French accent.

"I've obviously missed the joke," said Jane in frosty tones. Then she added, "Please tell me I haven't drawn on my face with a pen again?"

"No, no," gasped Dom. "Sorry. Please continue."

"Fine. In the next vignette, I am a colleague at the same professional level as you but run a different department. I blame you publicly in a group meeting for causing me to miss a deadline. In other words, I imply that you bottlenecked a project. How do you handle this situation?"

Dominic let her know with his body language that

he was becoming bored, since he was beginning to run out of sexy fantasy roles for Jane. He pushed his chair back from his desk, crossed one leg over the other and began to drum his fingers on his knee. He yawned. "Well, you know. If I really hate the guy, I just hide in the bushes and jump him when he comes out of the building that night."

At Jane's shocked expression, he laughed. "Kidding, Jane. I'm *kidding*. Bottom line, I will first point out publicly that if this is the way he feels, he should discuss the issue with me privately and not blindside me in a meeting. Second, I might explain that my staff had other priorities and that I was not consulted about the timeline for the project. Third, I could point out that our procedures are more complex than he has imagined. Et cetera, et cetera. I remain calm and do not lose my temper or fling accusations at anyone."

Jane nodded. "Okay, good. Next scenario." She hesitated for the briefest of moments, then took a deep breath. "I am an employee who is coming on to you. How do you respond?"

Dominic raised a brow. "Well, that depends," he said with a grin. "Is she cute?"

"How do you know the employee is female?" Jane shot back.

"Uh. Good point. I just assumed…. Anyway, I was again kidding. In a case like that, I'd certainly refuse to acknowledge the overtures. I'd pretend they weren't there. I'd make sure to *never* be with that employee in my office with the door closed or alone with the employee after hours. And if the behavior continued, I'd alert HR and make every effort to have the person transferred to a different department."

Jane made some more dutiful notes, and though he was doing his best to take her seriously—really he was—several more fantasy scenarios popped into his head. Jane as harem girl (his harem, of course); Jane as cheerleader; Jane as cave woman, clad only in shreds of tiger skin. The possibilities for fantasies about Jane seemed endless...and this was without him even trying!

Jane as fire woman, handling his lengthy hose. Jane as police woman, cuffing him, telling him gruffly to "spread 'em" and throwing him into her squad car. Jane as defense attorney, visiting him in his cell and, er, debriefing him against the bars.

She was speaking again. He had to focus, damn it. He was getting irritated with himself. It wasn't like him to not be able to control his thoughts, but something about Jane rubbed him—and not the wrong way.

Dom felt suddenly trapped behind his desk, unable to get away from her and this disturbing power she seemed to have over him. Not that he was sure he wanted to get away from her...an idea that made him even angrier.

There she sat, making notes about him as if he were a lab rat, and all he could think about was her naked? Jane and her prim suit and pink mouth and clipboard, wielding the power to get him fired. Why in the hell was he putting up with this? Why didn't he just slap his resignation on Arianna's desk and show her one of his best features—his ass?

The answer was simple: he refused to let her win. She wanted him out; therefore he'd stay in. And somehow, some way, he'd teach her that backstabbing, lying and cheating were not good ways to get ahead.

Jane was speaking again, sketching out another stupid vignette.

"What?" he snapped. "I didn't catch that."

She stood up and slapped her clipboard on his desk, placing her palms on either side of it and glowering down at him. "You didn't catch that because you weren't paying attention. And I don't know what I've done to create the hostility that's pouring off of you in waves, but a, I'm tired of it and b, it's not doing you any favors with me. First you find ways to turn my questions into jokes, then you get angry and finally you're not paying any attention at all. What exactly are you trying to achieve with this behavior? Should I write up my evaluation this second? Because you're sure doing your best to look guilty as charged."

Dom glowered at her and fought the insane urge to pull her right onto his desk and show her who was boss here. Man to woman.

Except the next image that popped into his head was of Jane straddling *him*. Who'd show whom? Christ. He rubbed a hand over his face and pushed back from the desk.

"I don't know what's wrong with me," he muttered. He looked up, met her eyes and still saw, with something akin to astonishment, understanding there.

"Look, Jane. I'm sorry. You're right. I'm being hostile. But I feel that I've already been tried and condemned. I think you've come in here with a lot of preconceptions and an agenda of your own. It's extremely hard for me to fight against that, and it makes me mad."

Jane said nothing for a moment. When she spoke, the words came out slowly and quietly. "I don't have any preconceptions or a hidden agenda."

He shot her a sardonic glance. *Bull.*

"Come on," she said in a sudden burst of energy. "Let's get out of this place. I don't think we're going to get anywhere with this in an office setting. You're too defensive here."

Dom eyed her warily. "Where do you want to go?"

"You play pool?"

"Do I play pool?" Dom snorted. "I have an uncle who makes his living at it. It's a genetic skill in my family."

7

THE THREE-LEGGED DOG WAS A mangy joint that catered to drunks and fleas, as far as Jane could see. Dom had probably brought her here to knock her off balance, but in reality it was no worse than the mildewed basement in which she and Gilbey had had their nine-ball battles. And hey, it took more than superskeevy shag carpet to intimidate her.

Jane stripped off her suit jacket, rolled up the sleeves of her blouse and requested a pint of any decent beer on tap. Dom lifted a brow and headed for the bar while she inspected the serviceable old pool table in the far corner, noting only one regrettable cigarette burn in the felt.

She found the rack, set it in the middle of the table and began piling balls into it. Jane loved the heft of them in her hands, the cold smoothness of them, the solid *clack* of them as they jostled one another.

She tried to focus on that and not how big Dominic Sayers looked in this tiny joint, how his head almost brushed the rafters of the place and his shoulders seemed to strain against the fabric of his very well-made shirt. She wondered briefly if it was tailored and more at length about the muscles underneath it. *Oh, Jesus, Jane! You're here to beat the pants off him in pool, not ogle him.*

She smoothed her hands over the fifteen balls in their triangle formation before her. *Pants off, pants off. Interesting phrasing, Jane!*

"You handle them well," said Dominic's sardonic voice behind her.

She jumped; glanced at him sharply to see if he'd meant any double entendre. But his expression gave nothing away. She took the proffered beer with thanks and tipped a healthy amount of it down her silly gullet. She needed to chill out and focus.

As she selected a stick, tested its length and weight and suitability, she felt his dark gaze on her. She fought with a blush as she ran her hands down the smooth, polished wood and slipped it back and forth, back and forth through her fingers on the felt. The thing was impossibly, inescapably phallic.

Resisting the urge to drop it and flee like a schoolgirl, Jane gripped it firmly and reached for more beer to calm herself. What was wrong with her? This whole venture had been her idea, her way of getting Dominic to relax away from the office.

Dom selected a cue for himself and then held it between his knees and the table while he rolled up his own sleeves. The stick jutted toward her at an outrageous angle and made her even jumpier. Jane gulped some more beer and inspected the barkeep's luxurious belly and extra chin.

Better to look at that than the way Dom's forearms flexed with muscle as he chalked his stick.

"You want to break 'em?" Jane prompted.

"Oh, ladies first, I insist."

She shrugged, ignoring the disturbing silk in his voice, and made her move. The balls scattered over the table, but not a single one found its way into a pocket. Embarrassing. And uncharacteristic for her.

"I knew you'd be a powerful ball-breaker," Dom said. This time there was no mistaking the double entendre.

She glared at him. "Yeah, well. It remains to be seen whether yours are solid or striped."

He grinned and raised his beer to her. "Touché."

She tried hard, really she did. But she couldn't not look at those positively sculptural buns of his. Especially when he cocked one hip to shoot. She should have been analyzing his technique. But no, her eyes remained glued to his glutes, at least until the *thunk* of him dropping ball into pocket snapped her attention back to the table. Solid or striped? Little ball or big? She did a quick analysis of the numbers left on the table.

"Striped," he said softly. "Big," he added with a devilish quirk of his lips. And then, after a thirsty swallow of beer, he said, "Long."

Jane reminded herself that these terms all technically referred to *playing pool*. Not to anything else. Her right hand tightened around her cue stick. With her left she drained her beer. Whew, that was fast.

"Nice…grip, by the way."

She almost dropped the stick.

"Experienced," he said inexorably. "Delicate but firm. Just what I like to see."

"You know what I'd like to see?" Jane asked.

He cocked a brow.

"Another beer, thanks." She dropped her empty glass into his hand and studied the table. Sure enough, he'd sunk the fourteen ball. It was a stripe, it was a big number and, to put it in that particular pocket, he had indeed shot long. *Still.* Surely she hadn't imagined that teasing, sex-drenched tone of voice. She wasn't stupid. She was trained to pick up on such things.

The man was flirting with her. Flirting with intent. The question was, why? Jane didn't kid herself that she was the sexiest woman on the planet.

The next question she had to ask herself niggled at her: why was she tolerating the flirting? Even responding to it?

Obviously he had decided to use his looks and his masculinity as a weapon against her. Obviously he thought her that gullible. She walked around the table, sizing up various shots, and Shannon's words came back to her. *Let him think he can use you for his own purposes.*

So…did that mean she should pretend to enjoy his attentions? Giggle like a schoolgirl and melt into a puddle at his feet? Sorry—it went against her character. *But…*

A slow smirk spread across her face; she could feel it. *Better wipe it off before he-man comes back with my beer.* She modulated it into seductive, subtracting the smug element that would alert him to what she was up to.

So Dominic Sayers thought he could play her, did he? Use her for his own purposes. Fine. Jane would play *him.* And if she got a…a…vigorous sexual experience out of the process, then more power to her!

Hussy, said her conscience.

Oh, shut up. It is the twenty-first century.

Sssssssllllllllluuuuuut.

Hey! It's not as if I'm dating anyone. And I haven't had any sex for, uh… Had it really been seventeen months now? Surely she was due some.

Nice. Your mother would be so proud.

She had no answer for this one—just pushed the thought away.

"Your beer," said Dominic behind her, the timbre of his voice tickling her eardrum. "By the way, that was a very effective dismissal. You neatly sidestepped the innuendo and reduced me from wolf to waiter."

She flashed him a sunny smile.

"Your gamble wouldn't have paid off, though, if I weren't a gentleman."

She widened her eyes. "I don't know what you mean."

"You damned well *do.*"

"Surely a gentleman doesn't curse at a lady."

He laughed softly. "I'm not *always* a gentleman." His eyes roved over her body. "And I'm willing to bet you're not always a lady."

Her mouth fell open and her pulse kicked up despite herself. "Take your next shot."

He set his beer down and did so unhurriedly. Elegantly. With a little English. He sent the cue ball high into the seven, which thwacked the ten into the side pocket and then spun the six into the corner hole. "See," he told her. "I'm an excellent…kisser."

Jane knew *kiss* was a pool term for contact between balls. She lifted her eyes coolly to his. "Yeah, maybe. But how's your follow-through?"

"Without equal." The words slipped from between very white teeth.

"We'll have to see about that."

Dom sank three more balls before he finally scratched.

She plucked the heavy white ball from the foot end and hefted it a couple of times in her palm while she contemplated where to set it on the table.

The subtext under the surface of their match wasn't subtle: the move was literally called *ball-in-hand*. She squeezed it deliberately and watched him inhale. After a long moment, she placed the cue ball exactly where she wanted it.

"The center spot." His teeth gleamed again, even in the low lighting. "So you like—" she watched him moisten his lips "—playing from the center."

Speaking of her center, did it have to throb like

that? Tingle? She ran her tongue over her own lips and nodded. She positioned the shaft of her cue stick and stroked, successfully pocketing two balls. She walked around the table, brushing past him (he closed his eyes) and sank another ball from the head. Then another. And another.

"You're gonna kill me," he said, taking a swig of beer.

"Oh, I hope so."

"You've done this before."

"You bet. I'm no virgin at this game."

"Little hustler."

"Oh, no—I never play for money."

"Just power."

Jane flashed him her best inscrutable smile, positioned her shot and scratched. Dom emitted a low growl of satisfaction, and Jane reluctantly ate her smile, inscrutability and all. *Darn it.*

In less time than it normally took her to tie her shoe, he'd sunk all of his remaining stripes and then called his shot on the eight ball.

Tough shot, thought Jane as she downed some more of her beer. *He'd be lucky to make it.* Without warning, two ounces of the lager unexpectedly poured down her windpipe instead of her gullet. Her lungs went haywire and forced the liquid back up with a vengeance—right as Dom stroked through.

The cue ball hurtled completely off the table as his stick hit it low down and center. It made a single dull bounce and then rolled under a couple of tables and all the way to the bar, where it hit a contractor on his paint-spattered heel.

The man and his two buddies turned and sent Dom a scathing glance, even engaged as he was in slapping Jane on the back. Their opinion was clear: what kind of moron sent a billiard ball sailing across the room?

Dominic scowled and *thwacked* her with a little too much gusto. "Are you okay?"

Jane nodded and panted, then resumed coughing.

"Did you—" *whack* "—do that—" *whack* "—on purpose?" *Whack.*

"No!" Jane was pretty sure she'd already coughed up one lung, but she tried valiantly to keep the other one down.

"Are you sure? Because you realize that you just won the game."

"I don't—" *cough, hack* "—play that dirty!" *Cough, cough.*

"But you admit to playing a *little dirty,* then."

Cough, hack, cough, hack, hack, cough. "Look, will you just get me some water?"

"Sure, if you'll promise to drink it and not breathe it."

"Bite me—" *hack, hack* "—Sayers."

He brought her the water, which she accepted gratefully. Once she was breathing normally again, she cleared her throat and worked up a good glare for him. "I can't believe you think I did that deliberately."

He pursed his lips.

"I suppose you're going to demand that we play that shot over? That's just *soooooo* convenient for you."

"Excuse me?" His eyes glinted dangerously.

She cleared her throat one final time. "How do I know," she asked, "that you're not taking advantage of *me?*"

He loomed over her, coming so close that she was forced to back up against the pool table. For punctuation, he slapped one hand on either side of her. She almost squeaked, feeling like a ball in a pocket of Dominic.

His jaw angled, his mouth swooped closer and he seemed to inhale her. *God!* What was the man going to do? Bite off her nose? Sink his teeth into her neck, vampire-style? Kiss her? *Oh, yes, please.*

His voice stroked her spine and tickled her ears again. "I don't need," he growled, "to take advantage of women. Understand?"

Um. Yeah. Message received, loud and clear. But…would he change his mind about that if the woman in question were to, say, *beg?* Again she restrained an unseemly squeak.

Dominic, satisfied that he had made his point, flashed her a wolfish grin and stepped away, leaving her bereft of his heat. Hoo, boy. Her heartbeat spiked in a musical crescendo and took off again in some sort of crazy Dixieland swing. If she were indeed a ball, one stroke from Dom's shaft would send her caroming all over the bed and into the rails.

Really, Jane—you shouldn't be thinking about

strokes from Dom's shaft. The whole concept left her a little breathless, even in terms of pool. *Mind over matter.* Especially when the matter is on the verge of delicious, decadent mutiny.

"I'll give you that game," Dom said, "if we play best of three."

"Hey, hey, hey! You're not *giving* me anything, thank you very much. You screwed up and I won."

Dom shot her a look that said clearly, *I know what I'd like to give you. And it starts with a big O.*

She squirmed.

"Fine," he said. "Let's see who wins the next two. And I think we should each bet on the outcome, just to raise the stakes."

"I don't play for money."

"You mentioned that. So what *will* you put on the line if not your wallet?"

She took a deep breath. "What do you want?"

"Oh, Jane. You know what I want."

"That's not a game to me."

He raised a brow. "You sure have been playing something. What is it if not a game?"

You. I've been playing you. But she wasn't going to say it aloud. *And you've been playing me. And God only knows where it'll land us, but I intend to win.*

"No answer for me, Jane?"

"I'll tell you what I'll play for, Sayers. If I win, you've gotta talk to me. You open up. You stop being hostile and resistant. Because no matter what you think, I haven't already judged and condemned you. I promise."

"Mmm. Okay—if you win, I talk. If I win, on the other hand, you have to kiss me."

8

KISS DOMINIC SAYERS? THE concept rattled around her brain like a pinball.

Oh, hey. I'll do that for free.

No, no, no, Jane! Be a professional. No sucking face with the clients. Bad idea!

"K-kiss you?"

He nodded. "And not just some little peck, either," he added. "You want me to open up to you? Well, I want you to open up to me." He shot her a grin that bordered on the lascivious.

She stared at him. They were getting into dangerous waters here. It was one thing to exchange a little banter, a few words rife with double entendres. It was quite another thing to... Jane gulped the rest of her beer just thinking about it. *Nope. No way. Not even.*

"Okay," her mouth said. "It's a deal. And since there's some question about how the game ended, I'll let you break." *Aaaack!* What was wrong with her lips? Had they really just agreed to this crazy bet? She needed to twist them right off and keep them in a jar or something. Under control!

With a satisfied smile he rounded up all the balls and placed them into the rack. His touch on them was confident, sure, expert. He almost caressed them, as if they were—

Jane looked away and swallowed, crossing her arms over her breasts. *Stop it!*

Dominic dispensed with the rack, lined up his shot and scattered the balls over the table like her runaway hormones. He sank the four and the five into a corner pocket.

Little balls, she told herself.

He shifted to the left a bit and sank two more. "I'm on a mission," he said with a disarming grin.

Jane shifted her weight from foot to foot. Was she crazy? How had she agreed to this? Unconsciously she pulled at her lips.

Clack, kerplunk. Clack, kerplunk. Did the man never miss? She was getting a tension cramp in her toes. *Don't miss. Please don't miss….*

He didn't. Two blinks later he was lining up his shot on the eight ball and casting her a mock-stern glance. "No choking, no sneezing, no cell phone rings. Promise?"

She nodded, forgetting to even be annoyed at his implication.

He shot. Game over. She'd never even had a chance.

Oohhhh-kaaaay. Now she had to fight for her life. Or at least her pride. Because Jane always won. As a teenager, she'd been neighborhood champion.

She smoothed her hair back from her face and dug in her trouser pocket for the rubber band she knew was there. Slowly, under his gaze, she bound her hair with it. Yep, she knew she could win. So why this sudden shameless desire to throw the game? She became furious at herself for allowing the thought into her head.

"I'll return the favor and let you break," Dom said magnanimously.

She nodded curtly.

"Just to allow you some shred of hope."

Her eyes narrowed at him. Then she set up and slammed the cue ball into the heap, watching with satisfaction as the victim orbs scattered to all corners of the table. Not a single ball found a pocket, however, and she almost screamed in frustration.

Dominic cut his gaze from the game to her hot cheeks, and his mouth curved.

Odious, arrogant man. He'd put some kind of hex on her, it was obvious. That was the only explanation for her lame showing today. Because she certainly didn't want to kiss him. Imagine! He probably let his tongue loll out like a dog's. Or the thing was forked. Or he was one of those men who drooled on a girl's chin. Repulsive! Just because a guy was decent looking—okay, hot—did not mean that he had any technique, not to mention talent.

Clack, kerplunk. Clack, kerplunk. Clack, clack, kerplunk, kerplunk. No, he couldn't be doing this again! He just couldn't be allowed to take the whole game in this humiliating fashion. He'd miss eventually. He'd…game over? No!

He shot her a look full of intent, and she laughed uneasily. "Heh, heh. Surely you're too much of a gentleman to hold me to our bet."

His grin was all shark. "You don't know me very well, do you, Jane?"

She swallowed and looked away.

"Perhaps I'm such a gentleman that I won't let you dishonor yourself by welshing."

"Heh, heh."

"I'll ask you one question before I claim my prize. Would *you* let *me* off the hook?"

"Heh." But honesty demanded that she shake her head. Honesty was just *hell* on a girl sometimes.

Dom propped his stick in the corner and advanced upon her. He grasped her stick, gently tugging at it, but she held on to it as if it were a spear and she were a Zulu warrior. She'd…she'd…stick it up his nose if he came any closer.

"Give me your weapon, Jane."

She cleared her throat. "No." Why did it come out sounding like a question?

"Yes," he said inexorably. "I think you owe me something, darlin'."

She stared at his mouth, and her grip on the cue stick grew tighter. Somehow she knew that there would be no drool issues with Dominic.

"Jane," he said, laughter in his voice. "If you wrapped your toes around that stick, too, I could carry you off like a nice goat or suckling pig. Stick an apple in your mouth and hang you over an open fire to roast for some pagan feast."

She choked. The darnedest things came out of this guy's mouth!

He bent over her, around the cue stick, and that mouth came inches from her ear. "I won't bite, Jane."

She shivered. Turned her head just a fraction, toward his stubbly male jaw.

"At least, not hard," he whispered. And his mouth found hers.

This time, to her shame, she *did* squeak. And worse, the squeak lowered into a whimper and the whimper into a bona fide moan. Because Dominic's lips were hot and firm and insistent…and parted her own all too easily.

The cue stick clattered to the floor unnoticed, and she gripped his shoulders to stand, because literally her knees had buckled on her, going defective for the first time in her life. Perhaps it had something to do with the way one of his arms wrapped around her rib cage and the other moved to the back of her neck, coaxing and massaging liquid heat through every nerve she had.

Vaguely she registered clapping and cheering in the background. *Huh?* And when Dom lifted his head and she could turn hers, they discovered the barkeep and all the contractors egging them on with whoops and hollers.

A hot flush spread over her neck and cheeks, and she closed her eyes. Mentally she threatened to return her knees to the manufacturer if they *ever* did that to her again. As for her idiotic larynx, she resolved to have it removed tomorrow. Her throat had never made such...such...*politically incorrect* sounds! Whimpering had long ago been expunged from the twenty-first-century woman's vocabulary. Oh, she wanted to die.

"Come on," Dom said. "Let's get out of here."

JANE HELD HER HEAD HIGH AS they moved past the leering contractors, who'd had a few too many and were urging them to get a room. Apparently they'd won a blue ribbon for Best in Show.

Normally she wouldn't have held Dom's hand, but under the circumstances she grasped it quite gratefully and clutched it even when the door shut behind them. Night had fallen while they'd been inside the bar, which seemed apropos, since he'd lured her to the dark side.

Jane was very aware of his body as they walked across the cracked asphalt parking lot to his car, where she let go of his hand. Immediately she missed the rough warmth of it; the texture of his skin. He must have seen the regret in her eyes, because though he disarmed and unlocked the car with his remote key, he didn't open the door for her.

Instead he backed her against it and took her mouth again in a hot, demanding, no-holds-barred kiss. Jane almost melted and trickled down onto the pavement as his lips parted hers again urgently and his tongue took over her mouth, establishing the rhythm and possession that he wanted elsewhere in her body. He tasted of beer and something spicy—hot cinnamon?—and one hundred percent turned-on male.

A whole series of quick sexual shocks electrified her, shook up her nerves and ignited them with pleasure. Mad rushes of sensation shot from the tips of her breasts to her lower belly and between her thighs.

Dominic molded himself against her body, his erection hard against her belly and burning to go lower, seek her core, penetrate and stroke and pleasure her.

Her breasts had grown heavy and ached to be touched, played with, suckled—even bitten. As if she'd said it aloud, Dom's hands moved from her face to cup her there, lifting and squeezing until she went weak and rubbed shamelessly against him.

Then somehow her blouse was half-open and his tongue descended into her bra, his hands pulling it away from her flesh. She almost collapsed with the sensation as he found her nipple and devoured it, sucking as if he couldn't get enough.

Before she knew it, the rest of her blouse was undone and her bra unhooked while he suckled her other breast, and pleasure had her whimpering again into his dark, curly hair. She lost her sense of time or place; nothing existed but him, her and sensation.

She could have blamed it all on the beer, but she would have been lying. When he lifted his head, she kissed him hungrily again on the mouth, feeling his male stubble scrape around her mouth and chin; it burned her skin like desire. Again his tongue thrust between her teeth and explored inside, dancing with her own tongue; mating with it.

He withdrew slightly, biting her lower lip and then sucking it in possessively, releasing and then nipping it a second time. He brushed his lips to the side of hers, along her jaw to her ear, which he invaded and enjoyed, too.

A deep shiver ran down her spine as she felt his tongue in the delicate whorls, his breath warm and sensual. Then her lobe was in his mouth, along with her earring, and she could hear little metallic clinks as it came into contact with his teeth.

Relentless, his lips traveled from there down the side of her neck and into the hollow at her throat; down again to the top slopes of her breasts. Here he lingered and nuzzled before taking them into his large, capable hands once again and kneading until she wanted to cry out.

Her hands, restless for something to do, sought out the thick, hard length of him against her belly.

He went rigid and his breathing came faster. His palms pressed her breasts inward until they met and then his thumbs began to move in slow circles directly on top of her nipples.

Jane let a whimper escape and closed her hand around his cock. He shut his eyes, then opened them and gazed at her with heavy, half-closed lids, continuing to tease and pleasure her breasts.

She moved her palm along the full, impressive length of him, which strained against his fly, and he groaned. His mouth swooped down again to her nipples, and her knees began to shake uncontrollably. She gasped as she felt his hand cup her bottom, the tips of his fingers moving along the cleft of her buttocks and then inward until he tickled and teased her mons from behind.

Jane helplessly moved against the pressure, her body becoming loose and moist. Unaware she'd been holding her breath, she released it in a slow, ragged exhale.

She gasped again as his hand plunged inside her slacks and then panties, massaging her bare cheeks but trapped by her waistband and prevented from going lower. With a growl, his other hand left her breast and made quick work of her fly. Then he was inside her panties, cupping her and stroking her, parting her with a strong, sure finger that quickly found her most secret spot and teased it relentlessly.

Somewhere in the back of her mind, Jane was conscious of the Jaguar's door handle pressing into her backside and the window glass cool and hard against her spine as she jerked at his touch, tension coiling within her, tighter and tighter.

The night air was cool—even cold—on her aching, swollen nipples as he abandoned them for her mouth again, his fingers sliding inside her just as his tongue licked between her lips and plunged to meet hers. As they broke the kiss, she helplessly arched her back and moved to take his fingers deeper, and yet deeper still.

His lips closed over one of her breasts again, and the sudden warmth after the chill, and the delicious suction, was almost too much to take. She felt herself climbing to that mysterious metaphysical height from which a woman falls to orgasm, closed her eyes and thought, *Yes! Finally!*

Too close by, the door of the Three-Legged Dog crashed open and two beer-soaked contractors stumbled out, laughing and swearing at each other.

Jane and Dominic froze, snapped back to reality. He straightened and stood solidly in front of her to protect her from their eyes. She clutched her shirt together and zipped up her pants in record time.

To the casual observer they were two people just making out by a parked car. But the contractors recognized them from inside.

"Ain't you two got a room yet?" shouted one.

The other one laughed and made a rude gesture: thumb and forefinger of one hand forming a circle while he poked the index finger of his other hand through it repeatedly.

Dominic ignored them. If he took one step away from Jane, he'd expose her state of disarray.

Finally they got into their trucks and roared away.

Jane's face burned as if someone had held every inch of it to an industrial sander.

Dominic raked a hand through his hair and released a tense breath. He opened the door for her, and she slid into the luxury of the Jaguar's buttery leather seats, beginning immediately to fasten her bra and button her shirt.

Still in a state of confusion, she didn't question the idiosyncrasy of a man who drove an expensive British import but frequented seedy, mangy bars like the Three-Legged Dog.

Dominic got into the car himself, started the engine and began to drive, still sporting quite a stiffie.

Jane sat in heated, embarrassed silence until she noticed that they weren't heading back to her car. "Uh, Sayers? Zantyne's in the complete opposite direction."

"I'm taking you to dinner."

Jane absorbed this. "It's customary to *ask* a woman if you can take her to dinner before actually doing so. She might object."

"Are you objecting?"

Of course her stomach chose that precise moment to emit a growl that was half lawn mower, half jungle beast. "Um, not exactly."

"Well, then, that's settled."

"Has anyone ever told you that you're a bit high-handed?"

"Darlin', better high-handed than underhanded. Don't you agree?"

"That's not the point," she said stiffly. "I didn't agree to a…a…date."

He stopped for a traffic light, turned toward her and smiled. "And yet you're such a hot one."

"Whoa," Jane said. *Dom thinks I'm hot.* But she

said, "I think we just, um, got carried away out there. You really shouldn't talk to me like that."

"Mmm? Well, I don't think you should kiss me or touch me like that if you don't want me to talk to you like that."

Her cheeks caught fire for—what?—the tenth time that night? But she wasn't giving up. "I didn't actually kiss you. You kissed me."

"Yeah," he said in a dry voice. "And I noticed that you kicked and screamed and broke a chair over my head."

"If you were a gentleman, you wouldn't point that out."

Dom sighed and shook his head. "You know, we've *had* this 'gentleman' conversation."

Ooooooh! "You know what? I *don't* want to have dinner with you."

"Do, too."

"Do not!"

Dominic, blast him, began to laugh. Then he called her "chicken."

Jane pointed out, with any dignity that she could still scrape together, that she was not a chicken.

"I know," he said. "Because you're coming to dinner with me. You're not going to run away from what you felt out there."

Jane folded her arms across her chest. "I didn't feel a thing, Sayers!"

"Liar," he said in agreeable tones.

She made a strangled noise.

"Want me to prove it? Pucker up, sweet Jane!" The car swerved dangerously as he leaned toward her.

"No! *Drive.* Just—drive, you lunatic."

"That's better. Now, no more fibbing or I'll leave you at Max's Downtown to wash the dishes after our meal."

Beyond words, Jane simply clenched her fists and stared out the window. Max's? Dom was taking her from the Three-Legged Dog to a four-star restaurant. The man was nuts, plain and simple. Would they go bowling for dessert? And whether he was nuts or not, she *had* to get things back on a professional footing.

DOMINIC PULLED OUT JANE'S chair for her, noting with approval that she'd taken her hair out of that grungy rubber band. Her dark curls flowed freely to just above her shoulders, and he had to restrain himself from running a hand through them. *Back off, now, buddy. You're trying to seduce her, not scare her off.*

He seated himself and accepted a wine list from the waiter. He glanced at Jane's face before he scanned it. Her firm jaw jutted in sharp contrast to her soft eyes. She was a strong, full-bodied woman with some spice and deep flavor to her. "Red zinfandel," he said.

"Excuse me?"

"Do you like red zinfandels?"

Her full, pale pink lips parted, and she straightened in her chair. "They're my favorite."

He smiled. *Good guess.* He looked forward to running the game at this table, too. He'd sink her every objection into a handy pocket and sweep her off her feet—and into his bed. Those little whimpers she'd made in the back of her throat when he'd kissed her and pleasured her—sexy as hell—had given her away. She was his for the taking.

Dom ordered an interesting Australian zin. They made small talk until the waiter brought it to the table, the requisite swirling/tasting was complete and their glasses had been supplied with ample amounts of deep ruby wine. He was preparing to make a toast to her when she preempted him.

"Order anything you'd like, Sayers. I'll expense this meal."

The romantic potential of their dinner wilted immediately. *Sneaky little psych major.* He'd bet she'd said it on purpose.

A change had definitely come over her. She lounged back in her chair and lifted her glass to him quickly before drinking. "Mmm. Nice choice. A little too oaky for my tastes, but quite decent."

His mood darkened. "First of all, you're not paying for this meal or any other while we're out together. Second, if the wine's not to your taste, we'll send it back."

"Oh, Dominic, really. We're past the millennium, which means you can drop the alpha-male crap. And there's nothing so wrong with the wine that it needs to go back. It's *fine.* Perfectly acceptable."

Alpha-male crap? Merely *acceptable* wine? *Ouch.* His seduction plans were going horribly awry.

Jane was supposed to be *under the spell of his male magnetism.* He'd had her at his mercy—he knew it instinctively! Where had he lost her? He had to regain control of the situation, get her all soft and mellow and turned on again. Damn it.

"So tell me about your background, Dom. Where you grew up, parents, siblings, all of that."

"Perhaps we could order," he growled, "before you start peeling my psyche like a cabbage? And I never agreed to talk to you, sweet pea. I won. You lost. Match over."

"Cabbage," she mused. "Interesting image. I think you're afraid I won't peel at all—I'll just chop your cabbage head right into coleslaw."

Cabbage head? The waiter interrupted his glare. "Ready to order, sir?"

"Yes. The lady would like—"

"The lady," Jane interrupted, "would like the shark steak, done medium. Thank you."

"The gentleman will have the lamb, rare."

"Very good, sir." He vamoosed.

"So," said Dom, swirling the wine in his glass, "you like to eat predators, do you?"

Jane smiled. "Oh, I just have a thing for sharks. I've got quite a few of their teeth on a necklace at home."

Dom would bet that was a bold-faced lie. She was just making a point; trying to tell him she had notches on her belt. "Really? You'll have to wear that to Zantyne one of these days. Arianna will think it's quite the fashion statement."

She narrowed her eyes at him, but he continued despite the warning. "What's the perfect foil for shark-tooth accessories? A grass skirt, perhaps? A top made of two coconut shells?"

"That's enough, Sayers. You can keep your chauvinistic fantasies to yourself."

"Oh, but that wouldn't be any fun at all. I'd much rather share them with you. That way maybe you'll invite me back to your place to view your lovely collection of shrunken heads."

"I'm not a headshrinker! I'm a behavioral psychologist and trainer. Can you cut me some slack here?"

"Maybe I'd rather cut off your slacks." His very white teeth gleamed at her.

Her eyes widened. This had to stop, and *now*. She'd gone crazy and let things get way out of hand in the bar's parking lot, God knew why. But enough was enough. "Okay, that's it. We are going to disregard what happened and be professionals here. One more sexual comment out of you and I call a cab."

"That's a shame."

"I mean it," she said.

He raised his hands, palms up. "Okay. No more."

She tossed back some wine. "And you can start telling me right now why you're using sex as a way to turn the conversation away from your main issue."

He felt his jaw tightening. "Which is…?"

"Being judged by women."

9

JANE LOOKED INTO SAYERS'S blazing eyes. His jaw was a block of granite.

"You are way off base, O'Toole." He drained the contents of his wineglass.

"Oh, I don't think so. Let me guess—domineering mother, quite possibly verbally abusive. Father not around much?"

"You are *so* over the line."

"And you weren't just now?"

He pushed his chair back from the table, tossed his napkin on the surface.

"Running away? What does a big, tough guy like you have to get intimidated about? If I'm so off base here, why not set me straight?"

He froze. "You're going to regret this," he said softly. "I can promise you that."

"Maybe." She couldn't help a shiver but refused to look away.

He sneered at her. "You really want to go there, huh? I suppose your professional instincts—and your vulgar curiosity—just scream for the information.

Well, why not, Doc? After all, you're so damned sure you know everything already."

She didn't blink, didn't back off, and his sneer grew more pronounced, but he began.

"One of my earliest memories of Mommy Dearest is of her tossing me up on a high-strung two-year-old thoroughbred, seventeen hands. She gives me the reins and then slaps the bejesus out of its hindquarters.

"I'd never ridden a horse in my life. My only emotion was terror, I can tell you—absolute terror. I hung on to that beast like a burr while it bucked uncontrollably and then galloped for miles, trying to scrape me off on trees, fence posts, even the side of a barn. You know how I dismounted? When the creature finally wore itself out, dropped to its knees and *rolled* on me."

Jane had covered her mouth with her hand and simply stared at him as he continued.

"Mummy and her martini thought it was fabulous entertainment—she laughed herself sick—until she had to rush me to the emergency room with several crushed ribs and a snapped femur. Simply ruined the rest of the day for her, I'm sad to say." Dominic poured himself some more wine.

"Then there was the sailing incident. Listen up, Jane. This is a good one! Mummy and her current beau hauled me out onto the Chesapeake on his shiny new J-35. No doubt she couldn't find anyone to dump me on.

"Somehow between the rumrunners and the sea

breezes, they got a little confused with the lines and ignored the threat of some incoming weather. So who got sent up the metal mast in a thunderstorm to disentangle the spinnaker line? Yours truly, aged twelve."

"Oh my God," Jane breathed. "Where was your father?"

"Not in the picture at all. He's some Austrian diplomat that she had a fling with. Never told him about me."

"Where was the coast guard? Why wasn't this incident reported to Child Protective Services?"

"It was. However, when your mother's family owns half the town, these minor incidents get swept under the rug. And of course, we moved…across several states to shack up with yet another gentleman friend. By this time, Mummy wasn't speaking to any of her family anymore and had finished putting her considerable trust fund up her pretty nose."

Dominic's face was devoid of expression as he spoke, as if he'd heard about these events on the local news. "Mummy had not been trained to do anything, of course, except party or get married. And her inherent sense of superiority over the 'masses' was not helpful in her search for or attempts to keep jobs. By the time I was fourteen, I'd taught myself C-code and was paying the rent on our one-bedroom apartment with contract software jobs. Mummy paid for her nose candy in more unsavory ways, while I slept either in the offices of wherever I worked or on the couch if I had to.

"By the time I was seventeen, I'd earned enough money to put a down payment on a house for her and get her into rehab. Finally I could realize my dream to get away. To go to college thousands of miles from there. I enrolled. I left her in Atlanta while I fled to San Diego. I was free—of her and of the programming work I loathed."

Dominic reached for the bottle of zinfandel and refilled both their glasses. He took a long draught from his. Then he laughed bitterly.

"But Mummy missed her 'good deal.' She screamed and ranted and threw rehab and her new job to hell. When I ignored her, she found a way to get my attention. She literally managed to set the house on fire when she got drunk one night. What better way to bring me home to take care of her? I mean, I have to hand it to her—the plan was brilliant."

Dominic leaned forward across the table, his eyes returning from blank and detached to blazing. "Do you understand now? Have you figured out why I'm allergic to manipulative sociopaths? I'm all too familiar with them, Jane."

She opened her mouth to say something—she didn't know what—but closed it again. There was no platitude in any human vocabulary that could make what he'd gone through okay.

The waiter chose that moment to deliver their entrées, and after a murmured thanks, she simply sat staring at hers.

"Shark got your tongue?" Dom asked.

She found her vocal chords. "I—I guess you could say that." She wasn't hungry. She wasn't sorry that she'd goaded him into talking…but she was shocked, in spite of all her experience. "Where is she now, Dominic?"

"Locked up," he said flatly. "Where she should have been a long time ago."

"In an institution?"

He nodded.

She poked at her fish. Without its teeth and sans menacing *Jaws* music, it wasn't much of a predator, was it?

She cleared her throat of an unexpected lump and blinked back threatening tears. Even the most dangerously macho man had once been a helpless, unprotected boy, subject to the whims of the adults surrounding him. A boy who must have loved his mother in spite of it all.

Jane opened her mouth and pushed harder without even meaning to do so. "You feel guilty and angry about putting her away, don't you?"

His breath caught, a harsh sound in his throat.

"You're furious at her for making it necessary—putting you in that position. Making *you* the bad guy, instead of her. It's not fair. None of it was fair."

Dominic closed his eyes before he got up in slow motion from the table. "You never quit, do you, Jane?"

She bit her lip.

He leaned forward, placing his palms on either

side of his cutlery. "Back. The. Hell. Off. Do you hear me, Jane O'Toole? This round is a draw. We're calling it a night."

DOM DIDN'T SAY A DAMNED WORD to Jane as they walked to the Jag. He opened the passenger door for her without comment, either, and closed it without one. He was furious with himself. Why had he talked to this woman? Had he been bitten by the stupid bug? She was the *last* person he should entrust with his past, for God's sake!

Sweet Jane, with her big brown eyes and her soft lips, had a core of steel and a notebook. She'd be logging every detail; using each painful shard of his history to create a psychological profile of him that suggested he had a problem with women. That he didn't like or trust or respect them.

And that simply wasn't true. He knew damned well that not every female out there was like his mother.

For one thing, there had been his math and later calculus teacher, Mrs. Borofsky. Mrs. B. had been the making of him, noticing his talent for numbers and constantly challenging him. Since she knew instinctively that he was bored in class, every day he'd pick up a special sealed envelope from her desk on the way out. It contained a "brain-buster" problem she'd come up with just for him. And every day on the way back into class, he'd slip his answer to her. At some point she'd find a moment to look at it and flash him a smile.

Dom had never received anything but that smile

as a reward or incentive for doing the work. But the smile in itself, the interest and the attention, meant more to him than just about anything in his young life. And close to graduation time, she'd let him know that she'd help him get a scholarship to any college he wanted to attend.

He'd also spent countless hours at his best friend Andy's house, experiencing the warmth and love that a mom should provide. The thought of Andy's mom was enough, almost, to make him smile at the moment. He pictured her lip-synching to Janis Joplin with a wooden spoon for a microphone as she made them the most incredible macaroni and cheese or meat loaf or brownies…. Renee was her name. She had wild, curly yellow hair; she was big boned and curvy and full of hugs and jokes. Her door was always open; her smile always inviting. And though he never mentioned anything about his own situation, she just seemed to understand.

Looking back on things, Dom thought wryly that she was probably glad her son Andy had taken up with a gangly computer geek instead of a beer-swilling hellion with a Mohawk and a nose ring. Christ, four thousand pans of brownies and countless of her husband's hand-me-downs were very much worth her peace of mind. Yet despite the cynical thought, he knew deep down that her affection for him had been real. He owed them a visit, Renee and her husband Al. He owed one to Andy, too.

As Dom drove, he noticed that Jane kept trying to

catch his eye, but he refused to meet her gaze. He stared straight ahead and focused on traffic. Several times she started to say something, but he gave her not the least bit of encouragement. She'd goaded him into talking to her; now she could damn well deal with his silence.

THEY RODE WITHOUT A WORD BACK to the Zantyne parking lot so that Jane could retrieve her car. Dominic's lamb entrée slid and crackled in its take-out bag in the backseat, while Jane held her shark on her lap. Shark in a doggie bag. It was incongruous somehow.

She stole a glance at Dom's harsh profile as he drove, and at his large, capable hands wrapped around the wheel. She tried not to think about how they had felt wrapped around her waist or stroking the back of her neck.

Dom's revelations about his childhood humbled her. She had expected a much less intense story of a demanding, unhappy matriarch who could never be pleased. But he'd been outright abused. He'd been through hell.

And based upon his experiences, it would be an outright miracle if he didn't have some kind of grudge against women. Your parents formed your earliest expectations about the human race. They shaped your worldview.

She'd won. She'd achieved her objective of getting Dom to talk about his past. But Jane felt more deflated than elated to find all of this out about Dominic. Even though it would make writing her evaluation easier.

Dom braked for a red light, and the plastic bag in her lap threatened to slide to the floor. Jane grabbed it and pulled it toward her. She couldn't help feeling uncomfortable with this whole situation.

Instead of feeling triumphant and validated that her hunch about his background was more or less correct, she felt…sick. She felt a little ashamed by how she'd gotten the information. And the manner in which she'd gotten it seemed to suggest that it stay off the record.

Dom had been trying to take her to a nice dinner. Granted, she was also quite sure he'd meant to seduce her. But hadn't she planned on seducing him right back? And what had happened to derail her from that plan?

Somehow she was unable to give up power for long with a man. He'd won the game of pool. He'd had her reeling under his kiss. And he'd had her scared and unsure of how her body would react to him.

She had *had* to get the better of him. That helpless feeling was just not acceptable to her. Why not?

Jane wasn't sure she wanted to know. It probably tied into one of her deepest secrets, the one she'd never share with anybody, the one she'd never cared to examine, in spite of all her training….

They'd reached the tree-lined parkway that led into the Zantyne building and the lot where her car was parked.

She gestured toward her not-so-new red Corolla, and he swung in beside it without a word. Then he got out, engine still running, and walked to her side of the car, though she'd already opened the door.

"Give me your keys," he said.

"Really, Dominic, that's not necessary…." but her voice trailed off as he ignored her and held out his hand.

"You'll have to tolerate my *alpha-male crap* only a moment longer."

She relinquished the keys to him and stayed seated as he got into her car and started it for her.

Then he helped her out of his vehicle and into her own. His eyes rested briefly on the pile of scrawled notes she'd left on the passenger seat—the ones all about him. But he didn't say a word more than was necessary.

"Thank you," she said, her voice awkward.

He nodded and closed her door with a thud. He turned away.

"Dominic," she said, rolling down the window.

His face was closed, his eyes distant. "Good night, Jane."

SUNDAY AT THE O'TOOLE household they ate fried chicken instead of shark. Courtesy of one Kentucky colonel, so nobody had to cook. This time Shannon came with Jane, wearing a hand-painted jean jacket and toting a six-pack of Miller Light.

"Is that a Chinese dragon?" Gilbey asked her. "Let me look at that." Shan turned for him so he could inspect the back of the jacket. Gil was one of the few guys in the world who would look at the painting and not Shannon's rear end. They'd all played too many games of cowboys and Indians, hide-and-seek and Marco Polo for him to be impressed by her looks.

Her dad, on the other hand, kept gazing at her. "Girl could be a top model," he said to Jane in the kitchen.

"She doesn't want to model," she told him. "It makes her feel weird. She doesn't like to take advantage of her looks. She feels that they're an accident of birth and just wants to be a normal person."

"I guess." He sighed. "You girls are all grown-up now. I remember you all playing around the house with your Barbies."

She smiled at him. "That was a while ago."

"Don't know where the years went. And now you have your own business. How's it all going? You turning a profit yet?"

Jane wanted so badly to tell him yes. But cash flow was always a problem. She'd be struggling once again to make their loan payment for the month.

"Well," she said, thinking about the lucrative potential deal with Zantyne and Arianna. "Business is really good, but it takes a while to get the numbers where they should be. Looks like we've got a deal in the works, though."

She felt...funny...as she said it. Dominic had told her everything she needed to know. All she had to do was log it in her report and give Arianna the results she was obviously looking for. So why did the idea make her queasy?

Her dad looked at her with pride. "You'll pull it off, Janey. I've never had any doubt that you'd be a huge success at anything you tried. It's just not in your nature to fail."

"Yeah," she said slowly. "Thanks." She hugged him and they went back outside.

"So, Gil," said Shannon, scooping up an extra-crispy drumstick. "Tell me about these sculptures of yours. I hear they're amazing."

Gil shrugged uncomfortably and took refuge behind a mouthful of coleslaw.

"They are," Jane agreed. "You have to show her after dinner, okay?"

He nodded.

"Did you contact Jim and—"

Gil shot her a look. "Yes. He took the slides. He had some recommendations about where to send them, too."

"Great. That's just great, Gil." Jane made herself shut up and crossed her fingers that her brother would actually mail out the pictures.

10

JANE SAT ACROSS HER DESK FROM Lilia and Shannon. "Okay," she said. "We've got to talk cash flow, scheduling and marketing this morning. So first I need you two to go over your receivables with me…."

The three of them discussed their billing and clients, upcoming presentations and seminars and efforts to bring in more business.

"When do you think you can hire a receptionist?" asked Lil.

Jane thought about Zantyne and Arianna again. "Soon, I hope."

"And a cleaning service," Shannon added.

"As soon as we can get our receivables outnumbering our payables—by a significant amount."

Shannon nodded. "So what's going on with the Zantyne woman?"

I was afraid you were going to ask that. Jane stalled a moment. Then she told them what had happened with Dominic at dinner, leaving out his more personal revelations.

"He sounds obnoxious," said Lilia.

Jane shook her head before replying. "Sayers is a man fighting for his career. He told me some things that give him motive for bad behavior with a female boss. And then he shut down. I can't really blame him. I'm the enemy. And I can't deny that someone's history has a great deal to do with shaping who he is today."

Lilia made a noise of dissatisfaction. "I wish you could spill the beans!"

"Yeah," said Shannon. "We want the real dirt on this guy."

"I can't tell you anything—you know that. It's a breach of confidence. All I'm going to say is trust me—he had a horrendous time of it as a kid. We're talking Mommy Dearest times ten."

"So you're right on target," said Lilia. "That should wipe out any doubts you've had about the boss lady."

"Yeeeaaaah," Jane agreed.

Shannon gave her a sharp glance and Jane avoided it. Her friend knew her too well. "Oh, would you just go ahead and sleep with the guy?"

Lilia's brows rose.

Jane blinked. "Excuse me?"

"It's very clear that you're dying to do just that."

"I am not! How can you say such a thing?"

"Honestly, Jane! You've been looking lustfully at *doorknobs* since Sayers walked into our office. How long has it been since you last got some, honey?"

Lilia gave up her struggle with gentility for once and laughed.

Jane glared at both of them. "This is not funny!"

Shannon winked at Lilia and Jane's irritation level rose.

"You cannot think that I would sleep with a client."

"Sure would help to get to know him better." Shannon grinned.

"No, it would not. It will only confuse the issues."

"Oh, it *will*, will it?"

"Leave me alone."

JANE SAT GLUMLY IN A LOCAL Laundromat, watching two different machines shimmy and shake. They held her clothes—the ones she could no longer wash at home for fear that the ruby-red lace tap shorts would melt into the very gears of her own Whirlpool appliance.

She had to call a repairman. She really did. But she dreaded facing him when he detached the lingerie. No doubt he would pull it out shred by shred, dangling them dubiously from a pair of pliers. Then he'd have a big laugh at her expense with all the other appliance repairmen at their local bar.

Worse, he'd see what size panty she wore! Because of course the darn *tag* wasn't stuck—no, it flapped handily for anyone to see. Anyone who happened to stick his head into her washing machine. *Jane O'Toole's butt is a size large!* the tag proclaimed.

Why, oh, why had she bought the damned things? What had possessed her to throw them into the wash without one of those mesh bags? And how much was she going to have to pay for the ultimate in humiliation? Eighty bucks? Ninety?

Hey, Mike! she could hear the repair guy saying. *Guess what I pulled out of some woman's washer this morning?*

The thought crossed her mind that her brother Gilbey could probably do the job, but a, he'd hang out for the day and eat anything not nailed down and b, she didn't really want Gilbey looking at her racy panties, either. Her father? Out of the question. There were just some things you didn't show your family.

The man across the Laundromat kept trying to catch her eye. The one who looked as if he hadn't showered in three days and ate live rats for breakfast. Jane carefully avoided his gaze and inspected her shoes. They were serviceable black pumps, the exact model of her serviceable brown ones. Boring, Shannon would call them. Jane called them comfortable.

She flipped through another few pages of the glossy women's magazine on her lap and wondered why she couldn't seem to look away from a human praying mantis—the model was that skinny—sporting hot-pink hoochie-mama sandals with silver stiletto heels. They were fabulous, and Jane did her best not to drool while reminding herself sternly that hot-pink hoochie shoes belonged in her life about as much as the Hope diamond.

A brief fantasy flashed into her head: she wore the pink heels, a zebra-striped micro mini dress and absolutely nothing else—for Dominic Sayers, of all people. Ha! His tongue unrolled like a cartoon dog's, lapping hungrily at her toes.

Yeah, right, Jane.

Speaking of toes, the praying mantis's little piggies were painted pink to match the sandals, and she dangled a tiny, elegant, hot-pink handbag only big enough to hold a lipstick and a bit of sin.

Jane glanced down at her scarred brown briefcase and grimaced. If she lived in Miami, perhaps she could mince around in sexy stilettos with a designer bag hanging off a manicured finger. However, she lived smack in the middle of Connecticut, where thick, woolly Fair Isle sweaters and rubber duck boots were always the height of fashion. Connecticut was hardly known as the State of Seduction.

Too bad. Because she really liked those shoes…. Jane tore off the praying mantis's foot, shoe and all, and stuffed it into her briefcase. If she weren't so sensible, she'd feel a retail crime coming on. But she was sensible, and therefore she'd resist. No visit to Beckindale's exclusive department store lay in her future. She'd just savor the photograph.

Her laptop winked balefully at her, reminding her that instead of reading mindless magazines and dreaming of being a sex kitten, she should be balancing Finesse's books for the month with her Quicken program. *Ugh.*

As one washing machine went into its spin cycle and the other made dubious thumping noises, she opened up the computer and pulled an envelope of receipts out of the side pocket of her bag. Lilia had offered to take over this task, but Jane preferred to do it herself. Even after years of studying effective management techniques, she had a hard time delegating. The irony didn't escape her, but she couldn't bypass her own personality, either. Darn it. Well, no one was perfect, not even her. Even though her ma had always told her she was. Jane smiled at the memory of being Mommy's perfect angel and shook her head.

If only her ma knew how much debt her perfect angel had taken on to start Finesse! Jane pulled up the Quicken software, her smile fading fast. The offices, their salaries, their health insurance, the cost of marketing. If Finesse didn't get some major business on the books soon, the bank was going to start heavy breathing down her collar.

Lilia had a group seminar on business etiquette coming up, as well as a gig to teach some eighth-graders in a private school. And she was advertising in the upper-end neighborhoods for cotillion classes.

Shannon was speaking to a women's club in Farmington and to one in Stamford. Then she had seminars lined up on several college campuses, one in a large sorority. Jane prayed she wouldn't forget to get rid of the weird nail polish colors, not to mention removing the pink streak from her blond hair. Shan was going to have to remember that this was not Los Angeles!

Jane could barely remember the three of them at age fourteen, dressed in their matching school uniforms. Surely Shannon had never worn drab olive cardigans, white button-down blouses and navy plaid skirts? Oh, and knee socks with loafers! But the past didn't lie.

Jane, today, came the closest of all of them to wearing that old girls' school uniform. She'd traded the knee socks for knee-highs and the loafers for pumps, but she still wore a uniform: the pantsuit. Okay, so she didn't own anything in plaid, but there were an embarrassing number of plain white shirts in her closet. Ditto white bras and panties.

Which was why she'd rebelled one day and sent off for the ruby-red lace. See where impulse had gotten her?

She needed a pair of pink stilettos like she needed a hole in her head.

Jane again avoided Mr. Rats-for-Breakfast's intense stare and began to work, fingers clicking busily over the keyboard.

Two plastic chairs down from her, a couple of older women gossiped about their neighbors, relatives and congregation members.

Across from them sat a wizened old man who was picking his teeth and, to Jane's disgust, sucking on the, uh, treasure trapped between them.

She prayed for her twin washing machines to do their job speedily and resolved to drag home wet clothes. Her dryer worked perfectly well, and she really wanted to get out of the Cash-Wash. Where were the hunky young guys featured on the C-W TV ads?

The ones who were clad only in their last pair of clean underwear and had to ask women for advice on water temperature and detergent? Talk about false advertising!

When the lurching and spinning of the machines came to a stop, Jane piled all of her soggy clothes into her white plastic laundry basket and tossed her briefcase on top. She lugged the heavy load past the gossips, the tooth-picker and finally Mr. Rats-for-Breakfast, avoiding his gaze for the last time. Keeping her eyes fixed upon a red sock in the basket, she bumped out the door with her behind. She was glad neither Dominic nor Arianna could see her right now, since she looked a lot more like a chambermaid than the CEO of her own company.

As Jane drove home, past the mini-mart and the dry cleaner and the gas station, thoughts of Dominic intruded into her mind. For the first time she considered whether or not she owed him an apology. She'd behaved somewhat like a terrier in the restaurant, cornering him about his past. And she didn't want to think about the fact that her behavior had been fueled by her own defensiveness. She couldn't just relax and let down her guard around Dominic Sayers. He threatened her—not physically—on some deeper, primal level.

She stopped for a traffic light and it hit her: she knew she couldn't manage him. He was beyond her control. She struggled with the revelation. *I am the ultimate control freak.* She didn't necessarily like it, but there it was.

Jane managed and controlled everyone in her life, especially the men in her family. She'd had to hold them together emotionally when her mother died.

I can't control him, and that scares me. Unnerves me. Worse, it drove her wild. She was always struggling for the power seat with him in the room. And he saw through it.

Dominic saw through her surface competence to the vulnerable woman underneath.

It was just hell on a woman when she couldn't keep her sphinx face.

The car behind her honked, and Jane realized she'd been staring into space, driving on Mars instead of Route 4 in Farmington. Dominic had her all tangled up.

She saw him as a boy in her mind's eye—a dark, skinny tangle of elbows and knees, at the tip of a twenty-foot mast in a thunderstorm, trying to untangle a spinnaker line.

She tried to imagine the kind of mother who would send her child up a lightning rod on a turbulent, thunderous afternoon.

She tried to imagine the kind of woman who would burn down her own house just to get her son's attention. Just to keep her gravy train en route.

Jane turned into her driveway without being conscious of how she'd gotten there. Her eyes were wet with tears. Oh, yes. She had an apology to make.

11

JANE HATED APOLOGIES. SHE went out of her way to avoid making mistakes so that she'd never have to offer them. Apologies admitted weakness. They revealed that you hadn't thought out what you were doing before you did it. Apologies really sucked.

She stared at her phone for a long time before picking it up, noting the fact that its white plastic surface needed to be cleaned. She found a bottle of orange-scented antibacterial spray and a rag and scrubbed every inch of the device. The automatic operator squawked as she attacked each push button, every little pore in the ear- and mouthpieces of the receiver.

"Please hang up and try your call again. Please hang up and try your call again. Please…" Then the inevitable annoying *bleep, bleep, bleep* until she had completed her task.

She put the bottle of spray away and tossed the rag into her laundry hamper. Then she stared at the phone again. No avoiding it or her conscience. She had to call him.

He answered after three rings, his voice deep and abrupt. God, that voice! Just the sexy gravel in it shot a tremor up her thighs.

"Dominic, it's Jane."

Silence. Then he said, "Yes?"

Not "Oh, hello, Jane." Not "How are you?" Just "Yes?" in the chilliest tone of voice she'd ever heard.

She swallowed and tried to unstick her tongue from the roof of her mouth. "I called because…"

More daunting silence. None of the flippant entendre that she'd come to expect from him.

"I called because I think I owe you…" God, why was it so hard to say? "…an apology."

He laughed softly, which set her whole body to "vibrate." "I'm stunned. Why?"

"I put you on the spot, forced you to talk. Backed you into a corner."

"Jane, darlin', you have *way* too exalted a notion of your own power."

She drew in her breath with a hiss.

"But thank you. It's very magnanimous of you."

"Look, if you're going to be a jerk about it, then I'm sorry I called."

"Jane." He'd dropped the sarcasm now. "I didn't say anything that I didn't want to say. What bothers me is why I wanted to tell you those things. *Hmm?* I've never told anyone those particular details of my childhood. But for some reason I told you. *You,* of all people." He laughed again but without humor. "I've played right into your hands, haven't I, sweet

Jane? Tell you what. You do exactly what you think you should with that information. But I'm not giving you any more. That was our last meeting. Have a nice life, Jane."

She stared at her squeaky-clean receiver once the dial tone hit her ear.

I am so confused. I have him by the balls, so to speak. Yet I just apologized to him. And somehow he's taken the power back before hanging up on me! What is wrong with this picture? He is so alpha male. He is so frustrating. And damn it—damn it!—he turns me on....

DOMINIC PUT DOWN THE PHONE and expected to feel relief. Jane O'Toole was now officially out of his life. He didn't care what the hell she wrote in her idiotic report. She could say he'd been raised by she-wolves, for all he cared. Arianna would be delighted.

But the relief he sought by banishing Jane didn't come. Dom made an omelet, cracking eggs into a bowl with ferocity. Of all the women on the planet, why had he opened up to *her?*

Why talk to a nosy, bossy woman who annoyed him and carried around a clipboard to record his every move? Why talk to Jane O'Toole, who had the dogged instincts of an Irish wolfhound and kissed like Botticelli's Venus?

Oh, hey—where had *that* come from? Dom wondered briefly what Jane would look like naked on a half shell and noticed that he was burning his omelet.

Smug little psych major. Attempted bet welsher. Sore loser. Uppity female, trying to pay for his meals when all he'd wanted to do was wine, dine and, er…supine her. Ahem. Whether it was in the coat-check closet, under the table or in the bushes outside. His intentions had been pure! Purely wicked.

Dom burned the other side of his omelet and tried to put himself in Jane's shoes. How had *she* felt? She wasn't stupid. She'd known what his intentions were. So what would he have done in her place?

"Okay, I'm a woman," he proclaimed in falsetto tones to his orange cat, Rusty.

Rusty appeared to wonder where his nuts had gone hiding.

Dom cleared his throat. "I'm Jane. And this brute has just kissed me, wants to take me to bed. It's a business relationship, Rusty. I shouldn't mix it with pleasure."

Rusty meowed in anticipation of some omelet, and Dom, who had slid the brown, crunchy mass onto a plate, threw him a piece.

"Do I give in to my womanly urges, Rusty?"

The cat sniffed disdainfully at the gruesome nugget in front of him and walked away.

"I guess that means that I do not." Dom cast a disgusted look after him. "Thanks, pal." He took a bite of the so-called food and wrinkled his nose. "Just like Mom used to make."

He made a practiced, Frisbee-like maneuver with his plate, and the disc of burned egg went flying into the sink. "No, if I'm Jane, I…put the brute in his place, refuse to let him buy me dinner and pump him for the personal information I need to do my job." He snorted in disgust. "I do not go to bed with him. I piss him off so that he…backs off. Aha!"

Rusty wasn't in the room to listen to his ravings anymore, so he spoke them aloud to himself. "*Shrewd* little psych major. She pissed me off on purpose."

Dom got up and rooted around in his kitchen cabinets for anything edible. He came up with Top Ramen noodles and half of a protein bar. Tragically, after all of this insight, he had to go grocery shopping.

He made a list, shrugged into a jacket and wondered whether he should have accepted Jane's apology.

JANE'S KNEES HURT, AND SHE HAD a blister on her index finger, courtesy of the toothbrush she was using to scrub the tops of her baseboards. This was what came of cursed apologies! She'd gone from being figuratively on her knees to being physically on her knees.

To be fair, she probably wouldn't have the blister if she hadn't been clenching the toothbrush harder than her teeth. Great. Shannon already called her anal-retentive. It now looked as if she'd gone and gotten manually and orally retentive. What would the good Dr. Freud say about that?

On second thought, she really didn't want to know. She already recognized that she was indulging in obsessive-compulsive behavior.

"Have a nice life, Jane," she fumed. "Oh, that's just perfect." Evil impulses urged her to run, not walk, to her computer and write up Dominic's evaluation this minute. *Rude,* she'd type first. *Stubborn. Pigheaded and pig-minded.*

Protective of his date even when he's furious. An unbelievable kisser with a mouth that could melt a glacier...

Yeah, wouldn't Arianna be fascinated to read that one. Jane sat back on her haunches and swished the abused toothbrush around in a bowl of sudsy water. Her lower back, neck and shoulders were screaming in protest, but she once again attacked the baseboard. Once Finesse was turning a profit and she could increase their meager salaries, she'd hire a personal maid as well as a cleaning service for the office.

Huh. Then how would she burn off energy when she was mad?

Sex. She'd find a boy toy obsessed with his pecs and take the edge off her frustrations that way. That was the perfect solution for a young, single, female executive. She certainly didn't need to obsess about annoying men like Dominic.

Boy, it still irked her that he'd beaten her at pool the other night. She couldn't even remember the last time somebody had beaten her! The loss stuck in her craw more painfully than the apology.

The more Jane scrubbed and fumed and thought about it, the more it bothered her. He owed her a rematch, whether he liked it or not.

Jane got to the end of the baseboard, stood up, dropped the toothbrush in the sudsy water and crab-walked to the phone. Her knees! God, her knees…the dirtbag would pay for this. She'd crippled herself for life, and it was all his fault.

She launched herself at the phone, and because it was already clean, she surged on to the refrigerator.

"Dominic!" she snapped when he answered, throwing a brownish bunch of celery over her shoulder and into the trash.

"Jane?"

"You cannot toss me out of your life before giving me a rematch at the Three-Legged Dog. I won't have it." She snatched an apple that was fermenting in the bottom of the fruit drawer and chucked it into the trash can, too.

"You won't have it," he repeated. Was that amusement in his voice? "Well, I beg your pardon. I should have checked to see if you were *having* it before I cut you out of my life. How rude of me."

"Yes," she agreed. "Very inconsiderate." *Cocktail sauce should not be green.* Slam dunk. *And what on earth used to be in that Ziploc bag?* How could she have let her refrigerator get this bad?

"Tell me," said Dominic, "why I owe you a rematch."

"Because I lost."

"So?"

"I never lose."

"Neither do I."

Silence.

Finally Dominic asked, "What if I tell you no?"

"You won't do that," Jane said with false bravado.

"I won't?"

"Nope. Because you'll wonder whether or not I'd have beaten you."

"Yeah. And that might keep me up at night."

"You're laughing at me."

"No, no—I'm considering this challenge very seriously. And I think I'll meet you, under one condition."

"What condition?" Jane asked suspiciously.

"If you lose this time, you spend the night with me."

Words failed her.

"And then," he purred, "we'll both be certain of what you're having."

She hated the sudden hot flash this caused her. *Arrogant SOB!* "You—you—"

"Shall we say seven? At the Dog. Tomorrow night. 'Bye, Jane."

She was left clutching a sparkling-clean phone, a slimy, blackened bouquet of parsley and a truly hideous possibility.

She'd never had an orgasm during actual intercourse. Her goal was to have at least *one* that way before she died. That wasn't overly ambitious, was it? And judging by her body's uncharted response to him, Dominic Sayers was her only hope.

AND THEN WE'LL BOTH BE CERTAIN of what you're having.

Dominic's voice echoed in her mind until Jane

wanted to explode, and cleaning the fridge did nothing to cool her off. She relived the scene in the Dog's parking lot over and over, try as she might to banish it from her mind. She felt Dominic's mouth, set off by sexy stubble, on every part of her body. Finally, in desperation, she headed for a cold shower to snap her out of it.

She turned on the shower spray, threw off all her clothes and left them in a very un-Jane-like mess on the bathroom floor. But she couldn't quite force herself to get into the icy water and waited for it to heat up.

Once inside, she slid the glass door closed and reached for her sea sponge and foaming gel, soaping her neck and shoulders. Dominic's face appeared in her mind and he grinned a purely wicked grin.

The sea sponge slipped off her shoulder and between her wet breasts, scraping along one areola and causing the pink tip to tighten, harden and bud. Jane closed her eyes and blocked out everything but the sound of the water sluicing down.

She stroked the sea sponge under one breast, around it and then back under the other one. They felt inordinately heavy and they ached.

Gently she touched her fingers to her left nipple, vaguely embarrassed at her actions even though she was in the privacy of her own shower. It had been so long…too long…and the episode in the parking lot of the bar had reminded her. It still tormented her. What if the men hadn't come out the door just then? Would she have been crazy enough to let Dominic take her against the side of his car? Lay her on the hood? Bend her over it?

The images left her breathless and excruciatingly sensitive to each droplet of water rolling down her body. She pressed her thighs together, but that only made things worse. She spread them and moved under the shower spray, sucking in her lower lip. She raised her knee and propped her foot on the built-in corner seat. But water was no substitute for what she craved.

Jane squeezed the sea sponge and almost unconsciously brought it down to her nipple again, circling it with featherlight touches. She turned to face the shower spray again and let her fantasies take over.

She felt Dom's mouth close around her breast...suck, lick, fondle. He was naked in the shower with her, pushing her down onto the built-in corner seat, kneeling between her thighs as he masterfully tortured her nipples.

And then—oh, my—he kissed and licked down her belly until he reached the juncture of her legs. He used a wet thumb to trace the line of her lower lips ever so gently, making her quiver from head to toe. He worked from the gently rounded top of her cleft to the lush, fleshy center and then all the way back, sliding slickly back and forth along her own personal Main Street.

Jane moaned and let her head fall back.

Dom now paid special attention to those ripe center folds, rubbing his thumb in delicious circles until Main Street was in danger of flooding. Her breath began to come in short pants, and she'd begun a small climb to the outer edges of ecstasy until he took away his thumb.

No! Oh, please, please, please. Don't do that. Don't stop...

She moved restlessly, seeking his magic touch, but when it came, it was on her thighs. His strong hands pushed her knees far, far apart, and then his face was between her legs, nuzzling her, kissing the tender flesh. She quivered again and then froze, hoping beyond hope that the kiss would go further.

Before she'd completed the thought, his mouth closed over the core of her and she cried out.

Dominic made a sound of male pleasure deep in his throat and pushed her thighs back even more, until she felt exposed and vulnerable to the whole world. He bent his head again and parted her lips with his tongue, lapping her as if she were an ice-cream cone.

She melted under the assault, forming small unintelligible cries in the back of her own throat.

He went on and on, circling with his tongue one moment, plunging it inside her the next, gripping her bottom fiercely and possessively until she had the sensation that she was filling with helium, expanding and floating, going higher and higher.

Dominic suddenly fastened on her clitoris and

sucked hard, as if it were a ripe peach. Jane exploded in a maelstrom of light and a rainbow of color.

She opened her eyes to find herself alone in her shower with her sea sponge and gel.

12

DOMINIC KNEW HE WAS BEING AN ass to Jane. Perhaps being railroaded out of his job brought out his worst qualities—but he couldn't seem to help himself.

Whether being an ass was a step up or down from being a pig, he didn't know. And to continue his present barnyard status, he was randy as a goat.

However, there was no way that Ms. Jane O'Toole would meet him tomorrow night at the Three-Legged Dog. She had far too much self-respect to allow her competitive streak to get her into that situation.

Too bad. Because Jane drove him crazier than any woman he'd ever met. She was a maddening, sexy, brown-eyed challenge and he wanted to eat her with a spoon.

Why was it that the one time in his life he met a woman with such potential, she had to be working for his worst enemy? The injustice of it made him want to growl out loud.

And if only Jane realized how she was being used. But Arianna was perfectly charming…for as long as it took to identify any weakness in a victim. Then she'd jab at the weakness, smiling, until it was red and irritated. Apply meat tenderizer, so to speak. And just when her prey got distracted, she'd lunge for the jugular and take him down.

Arianna was very, very good at what she did for a living—not work but human sabotage.

He got angry all over again just thinking about her. God, wasn't there some way to beat her without sinking to her level? Some way to win without compromising his own integrity?

JANE WAS AFFRONTED ENOUGH by Dominic's challenge—or was she humiliated enough by her own private response?—to march straight into the office of Arianna DuBose the following morning.

"You're right," she said by way of a greeting. "Dominic Sayers *is* impossible."

Arianna's diamonds glittered, while behind them she looked very much like a hornet in her yellow-and-black suit. "Well, Jane, I tried to tell you. But of course you're a professional and needed to find out for yourself."

Jane nodded while analyzing the peculiar nuance Arianna placed on the word *professional*. She'd swear the woman had sounded…condescending? Derisive? Yes, that was it. A hint—or two or three—of derision had tainted those four syllables. Jane's internal radar went up, even as Arianna aimed a friendly smile in her direction.

The smile was a generic baring of teeth and could

have been aimed just as easily at an assistant, a janitor or the woman who came to spray the office plants.

Jane sensed a disturbing disconnectedness about the vice-president—she looked right through Jane as though she were invisible. *Oh, she's probably just distracted over some business issue. She must wear a lot of hats.*

Jane did her best not to wonder if one of them was pointed and black.

Arianna's gaze sharpened now, and Jane almost squirmed, finding the fierce focus even more disconcerting than the wide-angle stare. "Listen, Jane. I'd like for you to think about working closely with our HR department here at Zantyne." She got up and closed the door.

"To be frank with you, this is a fabulous company, but we're experiencing some growing pains. We've got some bad seeds and some deadwood around here. They're holding up expansion and they're balking at R & D costs for a revolutionary product."

The hairs at Jane's nape stood up and moved restlessly, sending a frisson of dislike down her spine.

Arianna produced an intensely charming smile and bestowed it upon Jane like a gift. "I need that deadwood gone. I need those bad seeds out of here. And you know HR people…." She laughed.

Jane forced herself to smile in return, but her mouth and chin felt like old wood—petrified.

"HR people are so damned warm and fuzzy." Arianna bit out the words as if these qualities applied to criminals or terrorists. "They want to give everybody a second, third, fourth chance! For chrissakes, I don't have that kind of time."

"I understand."

"So I'd like to bring in an outside expert to help move these people out of here. I admire your style, Jane. I'd welcome you on board as that expert." Arianna named a consulting fee that caused Jane's eyes to bug out and noted her reaction with a smug smile.

Jane blinked in the hope that her peepers would return to their sockets. "I'm...stunned at your generous offer. I don't know what to say."

Her Hornetness beamed at her. "Say yes, honey." There it was again, that faint derision in her voice.

"I'll need to consult with my business partners, of course."

The wattage in the beam dimmed a bit. "Fine. But I'll need your answer as soon as possible. Can you get back to me by Friday?"

"Yes."

"Excellent." Arianna stood up, signaling that her visitor should now leave.

Jane got up and made her way to the door.

"Oh, and could you have the Sayers evaluation on my desk by Monday? I've been interviewing for his replacement and I've found someone quite promising."

JANE TOTED A TRAVEL-SIZE hair dryer with her back to Finesse and squinted once again at the hairy flower arrangement on the office coffee table. She found a nearby outlet and plugged in, switched the device on to low power and aimed.

Surely this would work! The fan had simply been too strong. But the hair dryer, especially on low, should eliminate the dust without blowing the petals off the flowers.

Lilia emerged from her office to investigate the cause of the noise. Her faint, exotic eyebrows rose almost to her hairline. "Should I even ask?"

Jane turned toward Lilia, keeping the appliance pointed at the flowers. "They're dirty! I've got to find a way to dust them. I think this is the solution."

"Are you sure about that?" Lilia's tone was rich and amused.

Jane turned back to her project and immediately switched off the hair dryer. In disbelief she noted that the remaining flowers were still attached to their stems. But the stems now drooped double, so that the petals dragged on the coffee table. The whole arrangement looked as if it had a bad hangover.

While Lilia's shoulders shook helplessly, Jane swooped down on the vase with a small shriek and tossed the works into the trash. "I give up! I hate the darned things anyway! They just collect dust!"

Shannon could be heard laughing from her office.

"Quiet, you!"

"I didn't say a word, lamb chop. Not a word." Cackle, cackle.

"While I've got you all here, I need to call a meeting," snapped Jane.

"An emergency session on…purchasing silk flowers? Or perhaps real ones?" Lilia grinned.

"No," said Jane with all the remaining dignity she could muster. She stalked to the hair dryer, unplugged it and wound up the cord. Then she threw it in her desk drawer.

"We need to talk about a consulting gig I was offered today."

"The Zantyne possibility you mentioned?" Shannon appeared in her office doorway wearing a winter-white top that looked like shreds of old granny slips stitched to a sleeveless men's undershirt. Of course it looked fabulous on her, whereas it would have made Jane look like a giant mop.

She nodded. "Yes, it's the Zantyne deal." She filled them in on the startling fee Arianna had offered her to serve as a consultant.

Shannon whistled. "That alone would turn us a profit this year. Unbelievable."

Lilia eyed Jane shrewdly. "What's wrong?"

Jane slumped into a nearby armchair. "What's wrong is that I'd basically be a hatchet woman brought on board to—and I quote—"get rid of deadwood." I'd be a hired assassin for Arianna DuBose—you've met her, Lilia."

Her partner's brows knit. "Executive Women's

luncheon? Purple suit, vampire-red lips, lots of diamonds?"

Jane nodded.

"She seemed very nice."

"She's nice with a purpose. There's something about her that gives me the creeps."

"Well, isn't that a scientific opinion," Shannon teased.

"No, really. Dom originally described her as sociopathic. I didn't believe him then. Now I really wonder."

"Dom?" Lilia's brows rose for the second time. "Sounds like you two have gotten cozy."

Jane grimaced. "Not at all. The man is—" She clenched her fists in her lap.

"Pond scum?"

"Nooooo. Not exactly. More like those plants that live half-underwater. Slimy but with patches of leafy-green."

"I'm sure *Dom* would be flattered to hear that." Shannon grinned. "And I still think you want him."

"Wrong," Jane retorted. "And not the topic of discussion."

"Anything you say, boss."

"So what do you think about the consulting gig?"

Shannon and Lilia exchanged glances. It was Lilia who spoke. "It's a lot of money, Jane. But if you don't feel right about it, then we'll back you up."

Shannon nodded. "You're the CEO. It's your decision."

IT FEELS LIKE A DEAL WITH the devil. That was the thought that kept running through Jane's mind as she drove home that evening.

Her mind's eye wandered to a setting which it did not have permission to recall. Slick brown tile, assorted beer advertisements, rows of tired guys on bar stools shooting the breeze or staring blankly at the corner television. The big barkeep with the luxurious belly and the double chin presiding over all the elegance in his T-shirt and grungy apron.

No. No, no, no and furthermore, *no*. She was *not* going to the Three-Legged Dog to meet Dom tonight. Her competitive streak was getting out of hand if she was even thinking about it.

Chicken.

No!

She was a grown woman, staid and responsible and chock-full of self-respect. How could she even think about meeting that man's challenge? If she lost, she'd never forgive herself.

If she lost, she might just have the time of her life.

No! Absolutely not.

Jane looked at her watch: six o'clock. Plenty of time to get home, shower, change into jeans. She even had time to shave her legs.

Pathetic. Woman, you are pathetic.

Why? After all, she was going to *win* this time. She just had to take control of the table first and maybe toss him a psychological curveball to throw him off his game.

Jane drove home humming and mentally pieced through her closet. Jeans? No. She'd wear something black. After all, it was going to be his funeral.

13

THE THREE-LEGGED DOG, IF NOT precisely hoppin', was well stocked with burly, belching men by seven o'clock.

Dominic bellied up to the bar and started making friends, since he doubted Jane would show up.

He'd downed a couple of beers with a group of housepainters by the time she graced them with her presence, causing cardiac arrests all over the establishment.

The four of them immediately forgot their fascinating debate over the merits of silicone caulk. Every male spine on the row of bar stools straightened, every pair of shoulders thrust back, every gut sucked in. Jaws slackened. And the barkeep actually whistled.

"Hello, Dominic," she said in husky tones.

Jane—*Jane?*—wore all black. Or rather, the black wore *her.* Displayed her. Intimately. Right down to the hot-pink hoochie-mama skyscraper sandals on her feet.

Dazed, Dom focused on her hot-pink toenails and then ran his gaze up every luscious, inky curve of her to hot-pink siren's lips. *Say something, you jackass.* The message flashed to his muddled brain, which malfunctioned. "You're late," said his mouth.

Her chin rose. "Yes. You have a problem with that?"

He slowly shook his head. His eyes moved from her lips to her breasts—gifts of God, swells of enticement, cruelly covered.

Dom lurched helplessly on his bar stool and forced his curiously rubbery legs to the ground. "I'm glad you came." *And I'm about to.*

She cocked a hip and smoldered at him. "You don't say."

Dom peeled his dry lips apart. "You're dressed to kill."

Her mouth curved. "It's appropriate for the occasion."

Oh man, oh man. She's here to lose on purpose! Jane had once again surprised him. He focused on a silver charm around her neck, the only jewelry she wore. The charm danced back and forth, dangling provocatively just above her cleavage, and glinted even in the dingy bar lighting. It was an arrow. It pointed down, toward everything he wanted from her tonight.

Dom ran a hand over his jaw and shifted from one foot to the other. Drops of sweat formed at his neck, under his arms, at the small of his back. Mother of God, she was going to kill him. She had indeed dressed for the occasion.

So it's true. Nice guys do sleep alone. As soon as he'd shown her who was boss and tossed her out of

his life, she'd come back apologizing and she now
wanted him badly enough to lose.

Dom grinned, displaying every tooth he owned.
"Well, then. Let's get this game over with." He turned
to the group of painters. "Excuse me, gentlemen."

Jane had already begun an unspeakably cruel sa-
shay toward the pool table in the back. That delicious
bottom of hers taunted him; begged to be peeled like
a ripe peach; beckoned him to sink his teeth into it,
then go lower and suck out nectar.

Dom wanted her so badly his teeth ached. He was
cold, hard steel. He could barely walk. Somehow he
made it to the table, thanking fate that a certain part
of him wasn't facing the bar, because there was no
disguising his arousal.

On the other side of the table, Witchy Woman
chalked her cue stick and didn't bother to be subtle.
The stick—*lucky, lucky stick!*—nuzzled her breasts as
she worked the tip thoroughly until it shone deep
blue. She met his gaze, then cast her eyes lower, registering the effect she was having on him. She smiled.

He gritted his teeth. Oh, but she'd pay for this!

"Shall I break?"

He didn't trust himself to speak; just nodded.

Jane racked the balls while he tried like hell to
look away from that evil little arrow shimmering
away between her lush breasts.

He summoned every ounce of willpower and refused to pant.

She removed the rack, stepped back, slid the stick

back and forth between her palms and nimble fingers. She bent over, the silver arrow dangling wildly, and Dom crammed his knuckles into his mouth as his gaze slid down, down, down. If only, only he were a Lilliputian! To tumble in utter bliss between those gorgeous, sumptuous breasts. To sink helplessly into their soft female flesh.

Oh, yes! He'd be Al in Wonderland, falling through the looking glass.

Jane's cleavage moved, and his eyes, visual slaves, moved with it. Registering why she moved seemed beyond him.

Ball after ball sank into pocket after pocket. *Lucky balls…*

"Dominic." Jane's voice reached him dimly. *"Dominic!"*

He blinked.

"Your turn."

"Oh, yes. Of course." She'd sunk stripes. His were the solids. He lined up a shot.

She bent over to see better, and that tool of Satan, the little arrow, winked at him. *Look upward,* he told himself sternly. *Up.*

Fuchsia lips, soft and pouty. Jane's little pink tongue darting out to wet them, just touching the cleft of her Cupid's-bow mouth.

Hey, man, you gonna shoot sometime this year? Machismo, always so useful, spoke to him. He let it guide him, shot—and missed, the ball mocking him from the rails.

"Oooh. Good try," said his female affliction, patting him on the arm.

Her touch sent a fresh wave of electric frustration zinging through him.

Jane walked around the end of the table, and he followed the arrow's symbolic instructions, dropping his gaze to her black-silk-encased thighs.

He wanted to drop to all fours and rub his cheek against one. He wanted to part them and bite into her center, tease her and punish her until she was calling his name and he'd had his revenge.

Naughty little psych major, dressed to kill. Using her witchy-woman powers on him. Showing up here to lose so that she could save face about wanting him.

Why couldn't women just admit their desires? Why did it embarrass her to want sex with him? Strange creatures, women. Coy. Inexplicable.

But she wants me, she wants me! She's not indifferent…she dressed for me to seduce her.

Jane's wrap blouse slid up a bit as she bent over the table again to line up a shot, and her low-slung black pants dipped down. He bit his tongue hard as a fuchsia T-strap became visible.

Jane wore a hot-pink thong.

As the image sank into his overheated brain, he vaguely took in the wildly improbable sight of the eight ball hurtling toward a corner pocket.

Expertly Jane sank it, wriggled lower into her pants again and propped her stick against the wall.

"Thanks for the game, Dominic," she said. And then she turned on her hoochie-mama heel and headed for the door.

14

DOMINIC GAZED IN DISBELIEF at the cold reality of the pub door. So did the round dozen of men lined up along the bar.

"Awwww, maaaaan," somebody said. "She smoked you and threw you away!"

"Ground you under her heel," said another guy, nodding.

"Stubbed you out in a dirty ashtray," added a third—quite unnecessarily, in Dom's opinion. He glared at them and they subsided.

Yeah, she'd made a brand-name butt out of him. He felt a lot like a Camel—one with a ring through his nose and a couple of dry humps.

Humiliation, hot and sour, shot through his veins, followed by cold fury. And then, unexpectedly, admiration. *Badass little psych major.*

Dominic leaned weakly over the back of a chair as waves of laughter convulsed him. Damn her, she'd turned the tables on him again.

He laughed until his ribs hurt and he noticed that the guys at the bar were collectively staring at him, shaking their heads. They thought he was a loon. That he'd let down the male team. They found nothing funny in him being bested.

He grabbed his leather jacket, slapped a couple of bills on the bar. Time to go. He'd taken two steps toward the door when it opened again.

Jane stood there, her dark curls blowing in the breeze. And she threw him yet another curveball. "Would you like to come, Dominic?"

He caught it gloveless and drove it home. "Why, yes. *Hard.* Would *you* like to come, Jane?"

THE ENTIRE BAR ERUPTED IN whoops and hollers. Guys knocked over their stools to high-five Dom and each other; clink bottles; pump their fists in the air.

Jane could have fried an egg on her face as she stood there mute, frantically trying to think of a—oh, God, a *come*back. *Pig!* But she richly deserved his response. No question about it.

He sauntered toward her, triumph on his face. She just had to, *had* to wipe it off. Her brain came through for her at last. "Oh, thanks for the offer. But I've already done that. All by myself."

The bar exploded again, and an expression of reluctant admiration crossed Dominic's face. She prayed to God that none of the patrons knew her father or her brother.

For the second time that evening Jane turned on her hot-pink heel and let the door slam behind her. Only this time he followed, and she tripped.

Dominic's right arm caught her—a ledge of muscle right under her breasts. He pulled her backward, hard against him. Hard against what she'd been toying with that evening.

His other arm encircled her waist, his hand hot against her abdomen.

"Going somewhere?" he asked and buried his face in her hair.

Jane's entire body began to tremble. She felt his stubbled jaw brush the tender skin at the back of her neck. His lips nuzzled the hollow at the base of her skull; kissed her there; parted the unruly hair. And then he licked, foraying with his tongue, exploring tenderly an area no man had ever noticed before. She shuddered with the simplicity of it, the odd intimacy. Her body shook again—every muscle participating—and Jane could taste her fear.

She knew without any further communication or touch between them that this one man would cause her to lose control. That he'd reduce her to blind, sobbing need if she allowed his lips to travel downward from her nape. She trembled, she fought with her body and her personality and her desire. And finally she ceded power. Jane placed her hands over his big ones. She drew one of them up to cover her breast. She urged one of them down.

Dom sighed into her hair and tightened his arms around her, pressing into every inch of her. Then he turned her around to face him, touched his lips to hers and took her by the hand. He led her to his car and drove them to his apartment.

DOM LIT A SINGLE CANDLE AND his gas fireplace.

Jane got a vague impression of simple Scandinavian furniture, modern rugs and state-of-the-art technology. She didn't have much time to take in her surroundings because Dominic was unbuttoning his cuffs and then removing his shirt. She watched him awkwardly, suddenly shy despite her take-no-prisoners outfit and brave words earlier.

He dropped his shirt deliberately upon the head of an orange cat that had emerged from under a sofa. The cat disappeared—a cooperative roommate leaving the scene.

Jane couldn't look away from Dom's chest— broad, solid, warm. He cocked his head at her and gazed right back.

"Drink?" he asked.

She shook her head.

"Okay. Excuse me for one minute." Dom left the living room and disappeared into what was probably his bedroom. When he returned, he held a tie in one hand and a box of condoms in the other. He dropped the latter on the hearth and put the tie in her hands. She blinked at it.

He took a step back. "If you only knew the things that I want to do to you, sweet Jane, you'd run right out that door. I'm afraid of losing control."

"Me, too," she whispered.

"I know." He stroked her cheek. "I know that about you." He turned away—she heard the jingle of a belt buckle—and he stepped out of his pants, baring a smooth, golden backside and the most muscular thighs she'd ever seen. All moisture vanished from her mouth, and her breath caught in her throat. The flickering light danced along his skin, bathed his broad back in darker bronze. She knew the oddest desire to lick his spine...from the cleft of his buttocks upward to the suave triangle of hair at his nape.

Something in the core of her began to melt, drip like hot candle wax into secret places.

Dominic turned finally to face her. Stood tall and proud and gloriously well hung in front of her. Then he stepped forward and extended his hands. "Tie them," he said.

"Wh-what?"

"If you don't tie them, honey, and *right now,* I'm going to make you pay for every second I've wanted you. Since the day I walked into your office. And especially for what you did to me tonight. Knowing your personality, I just don't think you're ready for that. Not yet."

Oh. My. God. The candle wax turned to lava and surged between her legs.

How in the hell did he know that about her? How did he know to talk to her this way? How did he know she wanted to run...but that she also wanted him to catch her?

"Tie my hands," he said again.

And she did. She wound the yellow-and-blue silk of the tie around and between his wrists, pulling the ends tightly into a knot.

He tested it and sighed with regret. "You got me." And Dominic surprised her all over again by dropping to his knees. "Kiss me."

She stared at him for a long moment. Then she walked to him, put her hands on his shoulders and put her mouth against his. She tasted him, bit his chin. She bit his lower lip next, and he retaliated gently, sucking her top lip into his mouth. A deep, guttural rumble came from his chest, and she swayed against him. His lips swept down her neck, licked under her silver chain, took the arrow into his mouth. It clicked against his teeth as he released it and moved lower to nuzzle between her breasts.

Almost unconsciously she untied the knot at her waist and slipped the wrap blouse off her shoulders, baring her hot-pink lace bra. He sat back and groaned, then buried his face between her breasts. She felt his tongue slip under the lace, pull it from her nipples, take one in his mouth. Her knees buckled and she fell forward, forcing him back, and he lay on the hearth, his tied hands now over his head.

"Bring them to me, darlin'."

She straddled him and unhooked her bra, dangling her breasts over his mouth until he drew them into the wet heat and to the exquisite torture of his tongue.

Her thighs, spread across his flat belly, gave way

and melted, and she gasped as orgasm ripped through her. "No…" she moaned. She'd lost her chance at a "real" orgasm *again*.

"Yes," he urged. "It's okay. Come to me Jane, come for me. We'll make more, honey. Lots more, bigger and better." He sucked hard again on a nipple and she convulsed again, shaking against him.

Pants…she had to get her pants off. He chuckled as she removed them in record time and straddled him again, rubbing against his erection, undone by the sudden plea she saw in his eyes. She rolled on a condom over him, then raised herself and sank down upon him, watched his eyes go almost blind. She rose and fell, rose and fell, climbed and shattered again—as did Dom this time.

The orgasm hit her without warning, ripped through her, shook her like a rag doll. It scared her senseless and so did he. Jane was on top, no doubt about it, but she'd never been more out of control in her life.

Her defenses returned with consciousness. Her thighs were heavy. And oh, God, she'd sounded like a moose in labor…what must he think of her? She was sitting astride the man as if he were a Harley, and the orange cat came out again and simply stared at her before retreating again.

"I should go," she said shakily. *Goal achieved.* So that was what all the fuss was about. Her climax with Dom inside had been deeper, earthier, more explosive than any other. She felt more vulnerable and exposed than she ever had in her life. She didn't like it.

His eyes opened and his gaze roamed over her lazily, resting appreciatively on her breasts, traveling down to her belly—she winced; it wasn't nearly as flat as his—and finally to the juncture of her thighs. She wished she could squeeze them together and hide that part of her. But he was somewhat in the way.

"I do hope," he said, "that you're planning to untie me first."

The alternative struck her, and she grinned, forgetting her self-consciousness for a moment.

His eyes narrowed and she relented.

"If you insist." Jane slid off him and bent over his wrists. A few deft movements with her fingers and he was free.

She crawled in the direction of her pants and fished the hot-pink thong out of them while he watched. She stood and slid it on, then bent for her pants.

"Don't even think about it," said Dominic, his breath hot and ragged against her bare bottom.

She squeaked as he bit her—not entirely gently— on the cheek. And then, using her thong as a harness, he pulled her to him and spun her around to face him.

He kissed her there, through the pink silk, his hands hot and firm on her bottom. His tongue danced against her and she couldn't get away—did she want to get away?—and her knees began to buckle again. Her thighs quivered. He lifted her right one, set it on his shoulder and slipped his tongue under the thong.

With a cry she fell back, but he caught her, spread her even wider, deposited her into a chair. He laved her until she was incoherent, begging, liquid.

And then he was inside her, filling her, stroking her deep within, her ankles on his shoulders and her heart in his mouth.

Just as suddenly he slid out of her, and then his hands caressed her breasts, cupping them, kneading them, squeezing them together so that both her nipples were in his mouth at the same time.

Please, she heard someone begging. *Oh, please, please, please...* And he was inside her again, sliding her back and forth, glistening and shimmering within her like a silver arrow. It sang along her every nerve, pointing dangerously toward her heart.

She was nothing but sensation and spirit and pleasure. She was the key at the end of a kite in a thunderstorm.

She was going to come apart well and truly this time, shatter to the ends of the earth—

And then he stopped, withdrew! "Look at me, Jane." Outraged, she did, because she had to focus on him in order to kill him. She opened her eyes and saw his own, her body still on the verge of delicious chaos.

"Do you really want *all* the power, honey? Isn't it good to give it up sometimes?"

She closed her eyes again. *I'll put him through a wood-chipper later.* She tugged on his shoulders but he wouldn't budge—just grinned at her knowingly.

"Say 'uncle,'" he demanded.

"I hate you."

His hand slid between her legs and she shuddered. "Say it, Jane."

"Uncle," she muttered.

He teased her with the head of his shaft, rubbed her with cruel intent.

"What was that, honey? I couldn't hear you." He slid a couple of inches inside.

Her orgasm stirred restlessly, just out of reach, and she squirmed, desperate for release. "Uncle," she moaned.

He slid in an inch farther and took a nipple into his mouth, sucked hard.

A rush of sensation lapped at her, but he stopped again.

"*Uncle!*" she shouted, and Dominic, with a diabolical chuckle, gave her all she wanted.

Lightning hit her—electrified her—and the wind took her away and wrapped her in clouds of sensation. A long time later, she fell to earth sated.

NEEDLESS TO SAY, SHE GOT HIM back. The process involved her mouth, a bottle of warm Hershey's syrup and much swearing on his part.

"So you'll watch *The English Patient* with me if I continue?"

"Yes, damn you!"

"You'll wash and wax my car?"

"Ohhhh. Huh? Sure…"

She laughed and licked him while he clutched her

shoulders. "And you'll dance around with my pink thong on your head?"

He answered with a string of heartfelt curses.

"Was that a yes?"

She loved having him at her mercy. Almost as much as she loved being at his. She might be the one currently on her knees, but he was helpless in her mouth.

Ooops. Not quite helpless. He was out of the chair and on top of her now, and within moments she *experienced* the sunrise as she watched it, still trembling with aftershocks.

Dom smiled at her and propped himself up on his elbows. He reached over to brush a lock of hair out of her eyes. Then he turned mock serious. "No sickening chick flicks. No car waxing! And no thongs on my head."

"But you promised," she teased.

"My testicles were crossed."

They fell asleep in each other's arms.

15

JANE AWOKE IN DOMINIC'S BED, with her head pillowed on his divinely warm shoulder. He smelled contradictory and wonderful: of soap and sex, deodorant and musk, heaven and homemade sin.

His sheets were soft against her aching, sated body and she didn't want to move. But consciousness drifted slowly into her sleep-fogged mind, and along with it came an unwelcome guest: remorse. She'd slept with a client! No, worse than a client—she'd slept with the subject of her evaluation.

There was low-down, and then there was subterranean! And Jane had to put herself in the second category. What she'd just done was unethical and unprofessional.

She opened her eyes only to behold another head on Dom's opposite shoulder. An orange, furry one with unblinking yellow eyes that stared into her own without the slightest embarrassment. The expression on the cat's face held disdain mingled with curiosity.

"That's Rusty," said Dom. "He's a little territorial, and you're on his preferred shoulder. He always gets the left one."

"Good morning, Rusty. Will you ever forgive me?"

"He'll think about it," Dom told her and kissed her. He dislodged the cat as he rolled and cupped her breast in his large hand. A perfect fit.

Even as she drew back, her nipple budded under his touch.

"Where do you think you're going?" Dom growled as she moved. A funny little spark shot through her body at the tone of his voice; the rumble of it from his chest. She still thrummed from last night.

Yeah, you idiot. And you'd better thrum right on out of here. "I have to go," she said.

He folded his arms under his head and eyed her lazily; moved his hips and popped a tent with the sheet. "Kum Fu doesn't want you to go." His grin almost melted her.

She swallowed. *You have to write a professional evaluation of this guy and you know what he calls his most private part! Worse, you got Kum Fu'd four times last night....*

"Kum Fu could shatter a stack of bricks right now," he continued.

She shook her head at him. "You better stick him in a bowl of ice water and get some pants on, because my car is still at the Dog, and I have to go to work. So do you."

"Spoilsport." But he got up.

She tried not to look longingly at his magnificent body, but she was a red-blooded woman and it was simply impossible. Those thighs of his...they'd been between hers last night. They'd pumped till she'd been delirious and she'd bitten his pectorals. She'd muffled her cries in the hollow of his throat. And she wanted to run her hands all over his body again....

No. What she wanted was a shower, a hot cup of coffee and a business suit that covered her from neck to ankles. Tailored. Severe. Gray. Dignified.

He scrubbed a hand over his eyes, yawning, and then marched naked toward the kitchen, past the floor-to-ceiling windows. "Coffee?" he called.

She grabbed the sheet off the bed and trailed him, since all of her clothes were strewn across his living room.

"Do you always brew it naked?"

"Yup. Dominic's Hot Naked Special."

"Well, I guess I can't turn that down."

"You want Dom's Hot Naked Eggs, too?"

"No, thanks. I've got to get home, really."

"All in good time, darlin'. You don't let me have coffee, I'll run us straight into a tree." She watched him set the glass carafe under the coffeemaker and switch it on. Then he strolled back out into the living room. He plucked her hot-pink thong from the hearth and twirled it around on his finger, grinning.

"Don't you care that the neighbors might see you?"

"Nope. If they've got nothing better to do than look into my windows, then my nudity is their problem."

Jane clutched the sheet to her breasts and wished she felt as free as he obviously did. "Give me that."

"I can't have it as a keepsake? A blackmail tool?" He waggled his brows.

"No!" She snatched it from him and balled it up in her hand.

One of the ridiculous pink sandals she'd bought on the fly at Beckindale's yesterday evening caught her eye.

What had possessed her? Jane moved around collecting her clothes.

"You're different this morning, Jane. Regrets?"

"No." She tossed her hair behind her shoulders and retreated into the powder room with her clothes.

Regret *is not the word*. She dropped the sheet and shimmied back into the thong, which seemed all wrong this morning. She eased into the tight silk pants. She snapped the bra and wrapped the blouse around her breasts.

A few splashes of water and the rub of her index fingers under her eyes took care of last night's smudged makeup, at least until she got home. As for her hair…hopeless. Her hair told the story of their activities last night, no doubt about it. She tried to calm it down but it stubbornly remained well and truly Kum Fu'd.

She slid the hussy sandals onto her feet and wiggled her hot-pink toes. In the clear morning sunlight the color seemed obnoxious and more suited to a nineteen-year-old coed than a CEO in her thirties.

When she emerged from the powder room, Dom handed her a steaming cup.

Jane accepted it and took a sip. Mmm, perfect.

How had he remembered that she liked a disgusting amount of both sweetener and cream? It unnerved her; almost alarmed her. Why couldn't he be like every other man she'd known—thoughtless, self-absorbed and in need of guidance from a good woman?

Dominic didn't adhere to any of her personality predictions. Though he certainly had a combative, difficult streak, he possessed an unexpected sweetness that surprised her. For example, she'd never met any man so unselfish in bed....

Drink your coffee, Jane. Okay, so you broke down and slept with the man. But that doesn't mean you should stand around mooning about it all day. He is a work project! This was a one-time aberration. He is soooo not relationship material.

Jane's first basic psych rule came to mind: never date a man who hates his mother. He'll hate women in general and take it out on you in particular.

She took another gulp of his coffee and disregarded the fact that Dom didn't seem to fit this profile at all, regardless of what Arianna DuBose had insinuated. Plus Jane had been doing her homework over the past few days, and the three other past supervisors of his whom she'd phoned didn't seem to agree with Arianna.

Dom came strolling out of his bedroom to interrupt her thoughts. He wore faded, snug 501s and an old sweatshirt and gym shoes.

"Sure I can't persuade you to shower with me before I take you to your car?"

The idea appealed to her more than she cared to admit. "I'm sure," she said, blushing at the memory of how he'd had a starring role in her shower at home.

"You're a lot more fun at night with a few beers in you."

She stiffened. "Well, I'm sorry that you don't like my sober, professional side. I suppose that's to be expected, though, given the circumstances."

He raised a brow. "I do hope I earned some extra credit points on my evaluation last night." He flashed her a tight smile.

"That's not funny!"

"No, I suppose it's not." He palmed his keys off the kitchen counter. "Well, at least I'll have gone out with a bang—pun intended." He strode to the door and opened it for her.

"What is *that* supposed to mean?" Jane felt fury ride up her throat just as more coffee went down.

"You know exactly what it means."

She set her cup down, stalked over and poked him in the chest with her index finger. "You're just so damned sure that I'm going to give you a negative report."

He nodded. "Yeah. Especially now that you feel guilty for sleeping with me. Your outraged conscience will demand that you rank me down and not do me any favors."

She wanted badly to smack him. "You seem to forget that *you've* been the one not doing yourself any favors. Besides, it might just surprise you that I've done my homework! You've never had problems with a single other supervisor. There have never been complaints about you from other female employees. In fact, most women you've worked with seem to *like* you, God knows why. So you might just be surprised by what turns up in my report, Dominic Sayers."

They got into his car and drove in silence to the Dog, where he got out, same as before, and started her vehicle for her. She was both touched and irritated at his old-fashioned, protective manners. "Thank you," she said gruffly as she teetered into the car in her ridiculous shoes.

"Jane, I'm sorry," he said quietly. "I guess I've misjudged you all along. I've been defensive as hell."

She looked up at him. "That's understandable." She waited for him to close her door, but he didn't. He leaned his arms on the top of it instead and gazed down at her, his expression inscrutable. "I'd like to see you again," he said at last.

Her body hummed at the thought. "I'm not sure that's a good idea."

"I scare you."

Her eyes flew to his, startled. Then she shrugged. "Yes."

"You're used to analyzing. Keeping that superior professional distance. You can't do that with me."

She pulled at the door.

He wouldn't let go. "May I have a kiss?"

His dark eyes melted her resolve, among other things. Slowly she nodded.

He ducked inside the door and tipped up her chin, caressed her cheek, cupped her jaw.

She was trembling before his lips even touched hers. Not a good sign.

"I'll call you," he told her. He didn't ask. And then he closed her door and watched as she drove away.

16

DOMINIC DROVE BACK TO HIS apartment deep in thought. What he'd thought of as a way to get Jane out of his system had backfired. He had a feeling she was going to be in his system for a long damned time....

He couldn't get over the woman he'd discovered underneath both the severe pantsuits *and* the do-me-Dom getup. The suits indicated rigidity, reserve. The do-me duds suggested a woman who would throw a guy to the floor and climb right on top.

Jane O'Toole was a big fake. She'd trembled in his arms like a virgin. She'd sensed that he saw through her act. She was vulnerable and soft as a kitten under all that don't-mess-with-me CEO crap. And what was more, she hated that vulnerability.

I've got you figured out, sweet Jane, and you don't like it. She'd come apart in his arms; had lost her distance and control.

He didn't know it for sure, but he had a hunch: Jane had had sex before, but she'd never been truly intimate with a man. Not like last night.

He wasn't sure she...respected men enough.

"That's it!" he told Rusty while he threw off his

clothes and got into the shower. As usual, Rusty eyed him as if he were insane. The cat would never understand why anyone would willingly get under a jetting stream of water.

"Rusty," Dom continued, "it's almost as if she thinks men are second-class citizens, in need of coaching, advice and training! She feels…not hostile toward us but benevolent, in an annoying, superior kind of way. And cat, she lost that attitude last night. Along with her clothes and her dignity."

Rusty jerked his tail a couple of times, as if to say "so what?" But Dom was sure he'd figured Jane out. The question was what made her that way. It was time to find out a little about *her* past.

Dom dried himself with a thick white towel and inspected the clear bite marks on his chest, grinning. "Damn, I'm good!"

Rusty's response was to drop into a hunch and hack up a hairball.

After Dom had cleaned it up and thanked his pet for the commentary, he dressed and went to the kitchen to scrounge some breakfast. He rounded the center island, and his Italian shoe connected with a small, black, rectangular object, kicking it into the baseboard below his dishwasher.

Upon further inspection he discovered that it was Jane's cell phone.

He looked up her address. Since it was on the way to Zantyne, he decided he'd drop it off to her before work.

JANE GLARED AT HER OPEN washing machine and rolled up her sleeves. She *had* to do a load of whites today and didn't relish the thought of going back to the Cash-Wash.

Maybe she was feeling combative in preparation for dealing with Arianna DuBose. Maybe all that sex with Dom had turned her into a tigress. But she was going to get those red lace tap pants free from the washer this morning or die trying.

Jane stuck her head into the dark maw of the machine and grasped a hunk of red lace. She braced her knees against the cold white metal and gave a mighty tug. Nothing. The fabric stretched a little but didn't come free.

She tried pulling in another direction. Tried twisting. Tried working it sideways, up and down. Who knew Vicky's Secret panties were made of such industrial-strength stuff? If she ever needed to climb out of her third-story apartment due to fire, she could make a rope of the darn things.

She set her teeth and pulled again. Finally she kicked the washing machine, only succeeding in injuring her big toe. "Aaaaaarrrrrggghhhh!"

She'd had it. She'd joked with Shannon and Lilia about a repair guy having to use a pair of pliers and a blowtorch. Well, she might not have pliers, but she did have stainless-steel salad tongs! And while she was fresh out of blowtorches, she had a nice long-handled lighter for candles.

Jane marched to the kitchen and got both items. *Enough is enough is enough!* She was *not* paying some repair guy eighty bucks to do something she could do herself.

She peered into the washing machine again and grasped the red panties firmly with the salad tongs. Then she clicked the lighter until she produced flame. *Here goes…I am a twenty-first century woman and I am taking matters into my own very capable hands.*

The nylon would melt, she was sure, and the tap pants would come free, and she could get on with her life and her laundry. Jane touched the flame to the panties. *There. See? It's working!*

Her doorbell rang. *Fabulous. Somebody has perfect timing.*

The machine was all metal, so there was little risk if she just ran to open the door and sign the slip for the delivery of a package she was expecting.

Jane set the lighter on the dryer along with the tongs.

On the other side of her door was Dominic. "Uh, hi. What are you doing here?"

"You left this at my apartment." He held up her cell phone.

"Oh! Thank you so much. I, um—"

"What is that *smell?*" he asked, frowning.

"Oh, God!"

"There's smoke coming from back there!" Dom pushed past her.

"Uh, it's nothing, really. I've got it under control—"

"Your dryer—it's gotta be a vent fire. Where's your fire extinguisher? Jane, *where?*"

She ran to the kitchen with him following and retrieved it from under the sink. She'd never used one before.

Dominic grabbed it and hurtled toward the laundry closet. "It's the washing machine, not the dryer!"

"Yeah. I know…"

Dom set off the extinguisher, dousing the flames with white foam. "Christ, that smell! What is it?"

"Uh—"

"How the hell did your *washing machine* catch on fire?" Dom looked at the salad tongs and the lighter on top of the dryer.

Jane squinched her eyes closed. "It's no big deal, really. Something got stuck in the wringer and I couldn't get it out, so…" She coughed.

He stared at her. Then he peered into the machine, holding his hand over his nose and mouth.

"Are you insane?"

She shook her head. "I didn't want to spend the money on a repair guy."

Dom grasped the salad tongs.

"No, no—" She lunged forward but too late.

He plucked what was left of the red lace panties out and stared at it. The tap pants were blackened, stringy, foam-covered goo, but the red lace was still visible in places.

Her face literally throbbed with heat, she was so mortified.

"Do you mean to tell me," Dom said carefully, "that you deliberately set fire to your washing machine?"

"No! I mean, yes. I mean, sort of—all I wanted to do was melt the place where the panties were stuck...." Her voice trailed off at his expression. "Give me those!"

He continued to dangle them from the salad tongs. "Red lace, huh? And hot-pink. Crazy as you are, I'd *really* like to see the rest of your lingerie. Preferably with you modeling it, of course." He shook his head. "Funny, but I'd figured you for a white-panty, white-bra kind of girl."

She hated that he was right. "Not at all. I have lots of interesting lingerie." She pulled a towel out of the dryer to clean up the foamy mess.

He took it from her and did the honors. "May I take you to dinner tonight in the hopes of seeing some more of it?" He leered at her.

"No," said Jane, alarmed because she didn't have any more and another trip to Beckindale's was not in her budget. She pulled the towel out of his grasp.

"I'll pick you up around seven. See, I'm afraid of my competition at the fire department. I've seen those beefcake calendars. I'm thinking you lit up your panties just to get a truck full of hunks and their, uh, *hoses* out here."

"Get out!" Jane snapped the towel at him, laughing in spite of herself. "I'm humiliated enough. I'm not even going to respond to that."

He shook his head and clicked his tongue. "Get out?

Now is that any way to thank the tall, dark, handsome hero who just rescued you from certain disaster?"

"I had it *under control*."

"Uh-huh. Say thank you, Jane. It won't kill you."

"Thank you. Now go away! I have to get to work."

He chucked her under the chin. "You are indeed a woman of finesse."

"Damn right." And she slammed the door in his face.

JANE SPENT HALF THE DAY trying to figure out what to say in her evaluation of Dominic M. Sayers and how to phrase it. She struggled with her own sense of shame as well as her self-interest. Just because Dom had brought her repeatedly to bliss did not mean she owed him good comments. Yet if she wanted Arianna's continued business, she understood that she needed to make negative ones. Either way, she felt sleazy and she had nobody to blame but herself. Could she be objective and professional in this situation? Somehow she had to find her missing integrity.

She wanted Dominic. But at what cost? She also wanted money and success. But at what cost?

Jane turned off her computer around two o'clock, fleeing to the mall and Beckindale's for some uncharacteristic retail therapy. She was feeling sleazy, so why not invest in some more sleazy underwear?

She returned to her apartment with several sets of bras and panties: electric-blue with yellow daisies; see-through leopard with neon-green trim; hot-orange lace; and bodacious black. She was two hundred dollars more in the hole, which scandalized her interest-avoiding soul, but at least she had come to a resolution.

A few sentences typed into her computer would guarantee that Finesse made a profit this year and would truly put them on the map. She owed Shannon and Lilia this contract with Zantyne. They'd put their résumés and savings on the line along with hers to start the business.

She owed them a receptionist. A cleaning service. The possibility of salaries next year. She thought about having to go back to her employee-assistance drudgery and the endless stacks of paperwork.

Just a few words—that's all it would take—to ensure that she never had to go back there.

But Dominic's face appeared in her mind, and every instinct she had fought a negative evaluation.

An insidious voice told her that if she didn't write it, Arianna would find someone else to bribe and get the results she wanted anyway. So what was the difference?

Bribe. Her mind returned to the word, the concept. The difference lay with her conscience. No, she didn't owe Dom anything just because they'd slept together. But she did owe her New England Yankee self the ability to look into a mirror without flinching. And she couldn't do that if she destroyed Dom's career simply to further her own.

JANE TYPED THE LAST SENTENCE of her behavioral analysis of Dominic M. Sayers and pushed back her chair, staring at the blinking cursor on her computer screen. *Are you sure you want to send this?* the cursor seemed to ask. *You're kissing off a whole lot of money.*

Money that wouldn't just go to her but to Shannon and Lilia and Finesse. Money that could go back to the bank and pay off some of their sizable debt.

Was she truly being objective? Had sleeping with Dom changed anything for her?

Again, she had no problem reading between Arianna's lines. Her business dealings with Zantyne would be over as soon as she signed off on this report.

The cursor continued to mock her. *You don't owe Dominic Sayers a thing. He'll meet you for a few more dinners, a little more sex, and then he'll move on. It's not as if he'll want a forever-after fairy tale because you took off your clothes for him.*

Could she honestly say that her perspective of Dom hadn't changed since last night? No.

But neither could she claim that Arianna's job offer helped her objectivity where Dom was concerned.

More than ever she was reminded of the subjective nature of her job. Could she stack certain facts against Dom, such as his rudeness to her, his combativeness and his troubled background with his mother? Absolutely. She could make all of those things work against him and write up a report that justified firing him.

On the other hand, she had his former supervisors'

words of praise, his protective, old-fashioned, gentlemanly manners and all the indications that he'd triumphed over his upbringing. She knew Dominic didn't hate women. No man with such an attitude could have made love to her so tenderly.

He'd teased her, yes. He'd promised to get his revenge upon her. But he'd punished her with pleasure only, never malice. Not once had he been rough. He'd even asked her to tie his hands so that he *couldn't* get carried away. He'd given up control, put machismo aside in the one arena where an insecure man would never do so—in the bedroom.

Dom wasn't insecure in the least. He had no problems ceding power to a female, as Arianna said.

Great, Jane. So when Arianna demands to see your documentation, you'll just tell her all of that, right? Log it down for the corporate records: Sayers is phenomenal in bed. Provides multiple orgasms. No problem with women on top.

Yeah. She could see that statement getting her a lot more work. Referrals, so to speak…

But you don't owe him anything, whispered her old success-at-any-cost demons. *He's not happy at Zantyne. He'll probably leave anyway, because he can't stand Arianna DuBose, and you'll have lost a huge consulting contract for nothing.*

The success-at-any-cost demons were only partially right, however. True, she didn't owe Dom anything—except her honesty and her professional best.

If she stacked the facts against him, she was no

better than one of those "experts" for hire in legal proceedings. The ones whose testimony regarding the "truth" changed according to whomever was paying them, prosecution or defense.

She did not want to work for Arianna at the price of her integrity. And she did not want to see Dominic after tonight—for fear her heart would begin to crave him as much as her body. She needed a controlling alpha male in her life as much as she'd needed those hot-pink sandals.

But tonight—tonight she planned a memorable evening. She'd let him play her like a violin and then take back her power when she left the bedroom in the morning.

17

DOMINIC HUMMED AS HE GOT ready for his first official date with Jane. Knowing that she wasn't planning to trash his character and aid Arianna in firing him made her even more attractive in his eyes. Go figure.

And he'd found her damned attractive before…irritating as that had been.

She was dedicated and thorough—she'd done her homework. She was smart—she'd seen through Arianna. She was sexy beyond belief. She was beautiful. And that hot-pink thong and the repartee were just the cherry on top.

Damn, I think I'm half in love with her. Maybe even two-thirds.

"Hey, Rusty," he said to his cat as he finished shaving. "The hot babe who shared our bed last night? How'd you like to see a lot more of her?"

Rusty meowed.

"I'll bet she'd give you tuna if you were nice to her."

The cat rubbed his head against Dom's legs and purred. He wasn't particularly nice to anyone but

Dom. In fact, he'd been known to hiss at women visitors and bat at their ankles.

He hadn't hissed at all at Jane. Just gave her the unblinking hairy eyeball. That was a true thumbs-up from Rusty, despite the fact that he didn't have any thumbs.

"You even shared my shoulder with her, didn't you, little dude?" The cat rolled to his side on the fuzzy blue bathroom rug, digging fast at it with his back claws. Dom always thought of *The Flintstones* when he did that, since the legs of the cartoon characters started rotating before they moved.

Just like Fred and Wilma, Rusty didn't move an inch, but his back legs whirred like an eggbeater. Finally Dom clued in to the non-verbal feline communication. "So you dig her, huh, little guy?"

Rusty went still and pricked up his ears.

"First one in a long time. I almost got sued when you bit Brianna in the calf."

The cat grinned at him for a moment, before the grin morphed into a large yawn.

"Yeah, you rabid little turd. No biting Jane. You leave that up to me."

HE PICKED HER UP AT HER apartment. The smell of burned nylon no longer permeated the air, which was a blessing. Jane herself smelled like jasmine and vanilla and oranges when she opened the door. He wanted to bury his face in her hair and lick her from ears to heels. However, that could wait until later.

"Hi," she said.

"Oh, yeah." He couldn't help his response. She'd piled her hair on top of her head, leaving dark tendrils curling in front of her ears. Tonight she had pale, sheer, shiny lips, and her smile rose over a lemon-yellow cashmere sweater. The infernal, torturous arrow rode in her cleavage again, amply displayed by the V-neck. She wore faded jeans and electric-blue toenail polish on her bare feet. Pantsuit Jane was nowhere in sight.

Impossible, but she looked even sexier than she had last night. Softer. More lush.

"Come in," she told him.

He followed her like a dog.

"Would you like a beer before we go?"

At his nod, she pulled two from her refrigerator and popped their caps off. She handed him one and raised hers in a toast. *Clink.*

"To you," he said. "You never fail to surprise me."

She colored faintly and drank straight from the bottle like a good Northern girl. He did, too.

She gestured toward the living room and he took a good look around this time, since he'd really only seen her hallway and laundry closet this morning. She had sturdy, comfortable furniture: an overstuffed cream couch upholstered in cotton duck; a faded blue chair that had seen a lot of years and held a lot of behinds by the looks of it; a lovely old mahogany coffee table, scarred from use. Magazines, books and newspapers everywhere—in towering but tamed stacks, neatly categorized.

Jane had a small television, circa nineteen-eighty-something. A stereo system of about the same age. CDs overflowed the mantel, displaying her eclectic musical tastes—everything from The Doors to Benny Goodman, from Mozart to George Clinton. At the moment Ella Fitzgerald sang moodily, throatily about love.

Above the row of CDs hung a modern painting of a woman with dark hair a lot like Jane's. Laughter filled her expression, her head thrown back, as she played a huge lime-green baby-grand piano. The dusky blue figures of two men and a woman lounged next to the piano, their mouths open in song. Yellow lamplight bathed the whole scene, and the woman playing the piano wore an orange dress with the sixties lines of young Jacqueline Kennedy.

"My mother," Jane said.

"Does she still play?"

"No. We lost her twelve years ago. Breast cancer. They found it too late."

"I'm sorry."

"Thanks. It's been a long time."

"How old were you when she died?"

"Nineteen. Sophomore year in college."

"You were so young to lose your mother."

Jane's eyes darkened. She shrugged. "You know, I don't think it matters how old you are. You can be seventy-four and it'll still just about kill you to lose your mom."

His hand tightened around his beer bottle, but he said nothing.

"You lost yours earlier than I ever lost mine, Dom. In all the ways that count."

He said nothing, just walked to her built-in bookshelves and studied various titles, as well as the photographs in front of them. Her taste in books was as eclectic as her taste in music.

"Do you ever see her?" Jane's voice was tentative.

Dom's shoulders tightened and knotted just thinking about it. "My grandmother sees her more than I do."

Jane sat down on the squishy cream sofa and gestured that he should join her. "What's your grandmother like?"

He smiled. "Tolerant. Serene. Sees the best in everybody—even her crazy daughter. Has the same hairstyle since 1959, a fondness for blue gingham and still not a clue that those five-leafed plants in my mother's terrarium weren't going to bloom into tulips one day." He shook his head.

"She'll take homemade muffins to her daughter, and when they end up being thrown at her, one by one, her only comment is that they don't make nearly the mess that the little banana custards do."

Dom took a long pull from his beer and started to laugh. "She still says her pretty little girl is just headstrong and willful. She took up with the wrong people, you know?"

Jane looked appalled.

"It's okay. Really. I didn't pull the wings off butterflies or shoot dogs with my BB gun. I damn sure didn't get into drugs or alcohol—I'd learned that lesson. I just avoided going home. I practically lived at a friend's house, and his mom treated me like a second son. I lost myself in heavy metal and played bass—horrendously—in Andy's garage." He smiled at the memory. "If you want to hear the worst rendition of 'Wild Thing' ever recorded, I still have our demo tape. The one that was going to get us a recording contract."

He looked around at Jane's living room again and decided it was neat, practical and interesting, just like her. He wanted to see her bedroom—and not for salacious purposes. He wanted to see where Jane slept, the place where she ditched her gray and beige suits and put on hot-pink thongs and blue toenail polish instead.

"What's with the blue toenail polish?"

She grinned. "It's me, isn't it?"

"Er, no."

"Influence of my friend and business partner, Shannon. She's very L.A."

"Ah."

"I borrowed the polish because it just so happens to match…something else I have on."

"Is that so?" Dom drawled.

"Yep." She set her beer bottle on the coffee table. "We've just been waiting for my toes to dry."

"So the beer and hospitality were for cosmetic reasons? I'm hurt."

"Yeah, yeah. Where are we eating? I'm starved." She retrieved a pair of shoes and slid them on.

Dom finished his own beer. "We've got reservations at Vito's on the Square."

FOR THE FIRST TIME, JANE marveled, she and Dom were having a normal conversation that didn't involve one of them trying to mock, best or outwit the other. She let wine and laughter slide down her throat while relaxation drifted lazily over her. They shared the best sautéed calamari to be found in Connecticut. They shared a green salad, too. And for dessert, cappuccinos with mouthwatering tiramisu.

When they returned to her apartment, she no longer cared about pride or who made the first move or who was on top. Neither one of them wore the pants, figuratively speaking. They shared the pants—and they took them off together.

Jane put on some slow, mellow jazz, and Dominic snagged a bottle of lotion from the bathroom counter. He coaxed her down to the rug and rolled her so she lay on her stomach with her head on a cushion.

She seemed uncomfortable and tried to tug his discarded shirt over her rear end. He pulled it off and she murmured a protest, covering it with her hand.

"Jane, silly, I can't give you a full-body rub that way."

She murmured something and blushed. The words he caught were *big* and *butt*.

He took a playful bite of the body part in question and she squealed and wriggled. He wouldn't let her go. "Stop," he said. "You have a wonderful, generous, delicious bottom. And if you insult it again, I'll have to smack it!"

Jane muttered something about political correctness and patronizing males, and he kissed her on the ear and told her pleasantly to shut up.

He smoothed the cream over her back, massaging it in wide, soothing circles, while she forgot to be outraged and sighed in pleasure. He rubbed at what seemed like multitudes of knots and tense areas, kneaded each one until it submitted and relaxed under his hands and she could have passed for a woman-shaped Jell-O mold.

He smiled and took full advantage of her lethargy, sliding his slick hands down to the small of her back, then the cleft of her buttocks and farther still. He spread them a little and worked his thumbs inward to her mons, circling and rubbing until she arched her back and moved against him shamelessly.

The sight of her that way was so hot, so erotic, that he hardened instantly. He replaced his thumbs with the fingers of his right hand and played her as she rocked and moaned.

"I want you," he whispered. "I want you *now*."

"Yes," she gasped.

He didn't need a written invitation. He quickly made use of a condom, then grabbed her hips from behind and drove into her with almost desperate urgency. She was tight, wet and matched him stroke for stroke. Neither of them could get enough, it seemed. He rode wave after wave of taunting pleasure, tension spiraling and building, coiling just out of reach.

Incredible, he thought. And then, *I'm not sure I'll live through this one*....

Beneath him Jane let out a low, sobbing moan and exhaled. "Oh, *yes*..." She arched her back in an almost violent spasm, then reached through her own legs to caress the root of him as she continued to orgasm.

Dominic jolted at the extra contact and spun instantly into his own climax, spilling heart and soul— and probably mind, as well—into the woman beneath him. With a weak, helpless curse he collapsed over her, careful not to crush her beneath him.

When they'd caught their breath, Dom nudged her onto her back and kissed her lips, then each breast, then her belly. She smiled and stroked his hair back from his forehead.

"You do things to me..." Her voice trailed off.

"And you do things to *me*," he replied, kissing her again. "I think you're going to kill me. But I'll die a happy guy."

18

MUCH LATER, AS THEY STILL stretched naked in front of the fire, Dom rolled to look again at the painting of her mother. "Tell me about her. Tell me about the rest of your family. It's your turn to open up."

"What do you want to know?"

"Everything. And I promise not to file a report about it."

"Low blow. That's my job." But she said it with a smile, and he took it with a smile. He stroked her cheek.

"My dad and my brother live together near Glastonbury, on about four acres. My dad's depressed and my brother can't keep a job. I try to whip them into shape when I go for Sunday dinners over there. Dad should be on antidepressants and Gilbey…" She blew out a frustrated breath. "Gilbey builds strange things out in the barn. I don't know what they are, but they're really cool. Beautiful. He says they're sculptures. Anyway, every couple of months one of my loser cousins shacks up with them, too, and mooches until I come kick him out. I'm not too popular with the cousins, but they're a bunch of potheads and I don't care. Dad and Gilbey have enough problems without taking care of them. And I can't deal with Fred's drinking problem, Bill's fourth bankruptcy and Chuck's child-support dodging on top of everything."

"These are three brothers? What's wrong with them?"

"Nothing. They just need to grow up. But they all hang out and underachieve together, so it seems normal to them."

"And your brother's the same way?"

Jane hesitated. "Nooo. Gilbey works hard. Just not at any paid job. He always gets himself fired from those, no matter what I line up for him. I guess next I'm going to have to send out slides of his sculptures and talk to gallery directors in New York."

"Jane, why is it your problem?"

She was silent. "Because. Because it always has been. Since Ma died. She was the one who held us all together. She told us what to do and how to do it— in the nicest possible way, you understand. Loving. But she was the general."

Dom traced her collarbone and bent forward to kiss her. "And you stepped right into her boots."

"Yes. I suppose I did. And when I didn't know how to manage a situation, I found a psychology book and learned how. I studied the grieving process and survivor's guilt. I studied motivation and positive affirmation and personality types. I kept searching for the answers to the human condition. Searching for control...trying to make our lives right again."

Listening to her talk, Dominic understood her underlying issues with men. There was not a single male figure in her life who didn't need help. And Jane had learned to step in and provide that help whether it was wanted or not. She was the mother hen in a brood of big turkeys.

No wonder she kept her distance and assumed control with men. No mystery there. He was no longer surprised that she'd been so aggressive at their first meeting. She was used to managing and directing testosterone, familiar with hostility and well acquainted with men who needed fixing.

Dominic decided to seduce her all over again, throwing in a special challenge just for her. A peek into Jane's bedroom had revealed a lovely old brass bed covered with a hand-stitched quilt. While the quilt was probably a family heirloom, he was less interested in it than he was in the headboard of Jane's bed. Yup, perfect for what he had in mind.

He took her by the hand and pulled her up from the living room floor.

"Where are we going?" she murmured.

"Somewhere I doubt you've ever been before. Close your eyes." She did as he asked. He snagged a dish towel from her kitchen and went to her.

"Trust me, okay?" He folded it, placed it across her eyes and wound it around her head, tying a knot to hold it firmly in place. Jane's breathing became a little more shallow, a little bit faster. Her hair glowed copper in the firelight, which bathed her skin in soft gold. She looked gorgeous and uncertain.

Again he took her by the hand and this time led her into her bedroom, where he lifted her and set her in the center of the mattress. Then he helped himself to the curtain tiebacks at both windows and sat beside her. He took one delicate wrist, murmuring again, "Trust me." He tugged it up to the headboard and fastened her to it, turned on by her quick intake of breath and her obvious reluctance.

"It's okay," he said. "I promise not to hurt you or to do anything that you don't like. We can stop at any time, Jane. Okay?"

She nodded and didn't resist when he walked to the other side of the bed and took her other wrist, binding it, too, to the headboard.

She lay there, his beautiful captive, and he smiled—not at her helplessness but at her trust. It heated him, undid him, made him want to bring her all the pleasure he could. But he wasn't finished yet.

Dominic walked to the foot of the bed, took Jane by the heels and gently spread her legs as wide as was comfortable for her. Her breathing quickened significantly and her whole body went tense. "Shhhh. It's okay."

He bound one ankle to the footboard and then the other so that she was spread-eagle. Then he returned to the living room for the lotion they'd left there.

"Dominic?" she called, her voice nervous. "Dom?"

"It's okay, honey. I'm just bringing in the camera."

Jane gasped, tried to tug her knees together and shrieked, "Noooo!" She'd never in her life been this vulnerable to anyone. How could she have given him this power over her?

She couldn't see a thing, couldn't move, couldn't avoid his gaze at her most intimate areas. She felt bare, exposed and completely helpless.

His footsteps came closer and his deep voice washed over her. "I'm kidding, Jane," he said. "Do you really think I would do that?"

His voice calmed her, even though she thrilled to it, as always. She stilled and shook her head.

"All right, then. Remember, all you have to do is ask me to stop and I will. But we're going to pretend that's not the case, okay? This," he chuckled, "is a little bit different from the kind of role-playing you're used to at the office."

She wet her lips, then swallowed. She nodded.

The timbre of Dominic's voice changed with his next words. "For right now, you are mine. And I'm going to do things to you you've never even dreamed of. I'm going to make you scream."

Just his words had her panting. But instead of a more intimate body part, he took her foot in his hands and began to rub lotion into it, working the muscles near the arch and the ball. His hands felt like heaven, warm and assertive and powerful. Soothing and titillating at the same time. She sighed.

And then he started to make love to her with his voice. "I've got a spectacular view from down here, darling Jane. I can see the taut muscles of your calves and those very cute knees…."

She automatically stiffened, knowing where his eyes would travel next, and embarrassed.

"I can see the tiny spasms of pleasure shooting upward and the way your thighs tremble. And I think it's adorable how you're trying to press them together, straining against the ties at your ankles. But you can't, can you, sweetheart? Because I've got you naked and spread-eagle, and in just a little while, I'm gonna to eat you up until you're bucking and writhing and you *beg* me to stop."

He leaned forward then, still massaging her foot, and blew a delicate airstream up and between her legs. "But even then I won't. I'm gonna keep eating you, keep sucking you until you go *wild*. Until you don't remember your name anymore. Until you get it confused with mine. I'm going to ruin you for any other guy, baby. No other man can make you come like I can make you come."

Jane felt a series of hot flashes break across her body; her nipples hardened and she felt droplets of perspiration break out between her legs. Nobody had ever talked dirty to her this way.

Dominic made circles at her arch. "I'm going to rub your breasts like this," he murmured. "Each one. And then I'm going to take your nipples into my mouth and suck hard, just like this." He bent his head, and his mouth closed around each one of her toes, tongue laving the clefts between them.

Ugh, she thought. *What if they're not clean?* "Dominic," she protested. "You can't do that—"

"I can do anything I want to," he purred. "Remember?" He laughed softly. "You're so cute when you tense up like that. Did you know that every part of you tenses? Even that sweet part of you—it frowns at me. Makes me wanna just nibble on it, just like this."

The breath hitched in her throat as she felt his breath *right there.* And then his tongue touched her— just a tickle, really—and she cried out, almost melting on the spot.

He chuckled, brushed the back of his hand across her belly and went back to the end of the bed, taking her other foot into his hands. Her thighs were trembling with need, and she ached for him to touch her erogenous zones, but he continued to calmly massage her foot and talk dirty.

"Your lips down there—pouting at me so pretty— they're ever so kissable, honey. Just peeking out, winking at me from their little hiding place. So hot. So pink. So good."

She was going to spontaneously combust if he didn't stop. Or didn't start. Or, or, or something.

"And the way your thighs blossom into those gorgeous little cheeks of yours, mmm. So round and soft and sexy—the way they curve around and tease me. I just wanna take a big bite right now."

The toes of her other foot were in his mouth, and

he sucked them as if he couldn't get enough. Jane felt the pull of his mouth in other parts of her, felt his lips everywhere, and she moaned.

He worked lotion into her calves next, hands moving slickly on her skin, gripping and manipulating her muscles. Slowly he came to the backs of her knees, then kneecaps and finally to her thighs, his thumbs circling and dipping higher, then lower in a maddening tease.

She stirred restlessly and he chuckled again. "What do you want, Jane? Hmm? Tell me what you want, baby."

She kept silent, though, ashamed to say it out loud. She wasn't the kind of woman who gave directions. Wait a minute. Yes, she was. Just not—not in bed, where it was easier if people just read minds. In her fantasies, the guy always knew exactly what to do before she even knew it herself.

But Dom wasn't letting her slide. "Tell me, Jane. If you don't, I'll just have to stop. Do you want me to stop?"

No! She shook her head.

"Then what do you want?"

"I want you to…" This was embarrassing.

"What?"

"I want you to…squeeze both of my breasts together and…put them in your mouth."

"Your wish is my command."

Oooh, did she like the sound of that!

Dom straddled her, cupped her breasts and suckled them, driving all coherent thought out of her head. She hummed with pleasure. When he finally raised his head, she was near delirious. "Now what?"

"I want you to…" She didn't know if she could say it aloud. "I want—"

He stared at her from under half-closed lids, breathing hard himself. "Come on, Jane. Say it."

She bit her lip.

"Say it!"

"I want you to go down on me."

He broke into an exultant, wicked grin and slowly backed down, between her legs. Then he bent his head to her.

She screamed—unable to help herself—as he took all of her into his mouth. White-hot pleasure rocked her body and pounded in waves to her core, bringing her release, but a relentless one, shaking her like a rag doll as still he wouldn't remove his mouth, even though she twisted and bucked and cried out again and again. Finally his tongue gentled her, brought her back down to earth with slow, calming strokes. She lay absolutely spent and understood for the first time why the French refer to orgasm as "the little death."

Though Jane couldn't believe that she'd let Dominic tie her up, she wasn't sure now that she wanted to be untied….

DOMINIC LAY BESIDE HER later, listening to her even breathing. He smiled in the knowledge that he had bridged her defenses, challenged her clinician's superiority and engineered her release of control. Jane was no longer analyzing or managing his behavior—she was reveling in her own. He loved this side of her.

The question was: could she put aside her background and her training enough to enjoy a normal relationship?

19

JANE AWOKE AT THREE IN THE morning with one of Dom's legs thrown over hers and his arm across her belly. It set off every alarm bell in her head.

Aha! Possessive, alpha-male behavior, even in his sleep. See, this can't go on. You've got to break it off now, before it gets too complicated.

The romantic side of her argued. *Aw, what he's doing isn't possessive, it's sweet and loving.*

Ha. A lot you know.

The sex kitten in her mewled, *How can you give up this guy's between-the-sheets techniques?*

Easily. It's been scientifically documented that romantic love, and usually frequent sex, die in relationships after a maximum of three years.

You are such a cynic. There are lots of romantic, sex-charged relationships out there.

Exceptions to the rule. And I won't be lucky enough to be an exception.

How do you know?

Go away. I have to pee.

Fine. But can't we just keep him around for amazing sex? Just for a few weeks?

No!

Jane slipped from beneath Dom. He stirred sleepily but didn't wake—just rolled onto his back and looked like a magnificent, snoozing Caesar. Even with his features relaxed, he vibrated power. He had an arrogant nose. His lips pulsed with sensuality. He was far, far too good-looking. Good-looking men always demanded their share of obeisance, and she simply wasn't up for kissing His Highness's ring. So there.

She headed quietly for the bathroom and went through the motions of relieving herself. Nope, no ring-kissing for her. She preferred nice, humble men who knew their limitations—like her father. He was sensible, stable and didn't demand too much from life. He'd been content to be ruled by her mother....

So what are you saying, Jane? That you want a man who kisses your *ring? Oh, that's fair.*

"That's not it at all!" she said aloud.

Great. She was not only talking to herself but now answering. Having entire conversations with voices in her head. This did not bode well for her sanity. She pulled her robe off the back of the bathroom door and headed for the living room, where she sat cross-legged on the couch, staring out a window at the trees illuminated by a streetlight.

Jane turned from self-examination to ethics. From an ethical standpoint alone, sleeping with Dom was wrong. She had to cut things off immediately.

Worse, she'd been weak. Weak to give in to him and weak to give in to herself. The sexual byplay between them had turned into a power struggle, just like everything else, and she had lost.

So what if she never had another orgasm during intercourse again? She couldn't afford to turn into a weak, mewling, moonstruck, malleable, mawkish, m—uh. She was running out of *m* adjectives and finally settled on pathetic. Yep, *pathetic* pretty much summed everything up.

She couldn't afford to turn into a pathetic, love-scrambled mess—especially over a guy like Dominic. He was a lot like cocaine in male terms. Not that she'd ever done cocaine. But she'd studied its effects and she was positive that Dominic was pure coca leaf for easily addicted women.

Now, back to that losing thing. She refused to do that either—not on a permanent basis. So she'd lost a couple of rounds and given in to her own sexuality. Big deal. That didn't mean she'd lost the game. It was time to take back the power while she still could.

I am woman, Jane told herself. *Hear me roar—* "Yaahhk!"

Someone had sneaked up behind her and kissed her neck. Jane screeched and shot upward. Her head collided with something hard.

"Uuurrfff. *Ow!*"

She then fell forward, ending ass-up on the carpet with her robe around her ears.

"If you hadn't just broken my jaw with your skull, I'd be admiring the view," said Dom.

"You scared the crap outta me!"

"And here I was, trying to be affectionate. Christ, woman!"

Jane jerked her robe over her bare butt and assumed a human, rather than canine, position. "Do you need ice?"

"If this is what a guy gets when he nuzzles your neck, how do you react to a good old-fashioned snuggle?"

She inspected his jaw, ignoring the question. "It's not broken."

"I'm asking a serious question here. Would I get a knife in the ribs, or your knee in my 'nads?"

She glared at him. "Depends on my mood. Now, do you want ice or not?"

Dom rubbed at his jaw. "Nah. But I'd sure like you to kiss it and make it better." He smiled that addictive smile of his.

She felt her insides going all soft and gooey, which was of course the evil man's plan. "Look, Dom, we've got to talk."

He looked at the glowing blue numbers of the clock on her stereo. "Now? It's 3:35 a.m. I can think of a lot of better things to do than talk."

"I can't," she said firmly. "Want some coffee?"

"Hell, no."

"Hot chocolate?"

He stopped rubbing at his jaw and began to look resigned. "Sure."

She padded into the kitchen, pulled out the milk and poured two cups into a saucepan. She set it on a burner of her stove and turned on the gas underneath it. Then she retrieved cocoa powder and sugar from her pantry.

"Oh, good. You make real hot chocolate, not the lousy packet kind with water."

"Of course."

"What do you need to talk about at 3:37 a.m. that involves you creating a diversion with the stove and a beverage? Are you going to do this every night?"

She stirred the warming milk with a wooden spoon. "No. Because this is the last night. It has to be."

He sighed and yawned. "Must you give me the kiss-off speech before 4:00 a.m.? Don't you think it's a little early?"

He didn't seem upset at all. She told herself that was good. She told herself that was excellent, in fact. She refused to be miffed that he wasn't hurt or surprised or angry—even if it did take a small toll on her ego. Jane stopped stirring and put her hands on her hips. "Would you prefer that I wait until five?"

"No," he said in the voice of reason. "I'd *prefer* that you not give the speech at all. But you will, being you."

"What does that mean?"

"You've got a whole load of excuses up both sleeves, Jane, and we both know it. Do you have them on index cards? Or did you memorize them, in alphabetical order?"

She gaped at him for a moment before recovering. "That's so unfair."

"Nope. It's true."

The milk was bubbling angrily now, and she slid her wooden spoon under the thin skin that had formed on the surface. The nasty stuff clung to the spoon. She turned off the heat under the pot, carried it to the sink and poured a little milk into each of the cups she'd set out. This turned the chocolate and sugar mixture into goo and enabled her to beat out the cocoa lumps before pouring the rest of the milk in. She gave a final stir to each cup and then handed him one.

"Look," she began. "I only have two reasons for breaking this off now, while it's still fun. And they are not excuses, okay?"

His eyes had grown hooded and his lips had flattened, but he listened.

"One, we are two very strong personalities. And in my experience—"

He snorted.

"—relationships between two extremely stubborn individuals do not work because each constantly seeks to control the other."

Dom sipped his chocolate. "Which keeps things interesting."

"Which makes things bloody in the long run," she corrected.

"What a cop-out. So what's reason number two?"

"Reason number two has to do with my professional ethics. I have never slept with a client. I've made a mistake with you, and the only way to rectify that error in judgment is not to do so again."

"How flattering," said Dom. "To be an error in judgment."

"Dom, you know what I'm saying…." Jane retreated behind her own mug of chocolate and avoided his gaze.

"Yeah. I know what you're saying. And I also know what you're *not* saying. What you're not saying is that you're scared of letting things go any further. And you're also not saying that you're afraid you're being weak. It's all very symbolic, Doc, if you think about it."

"Don't call me 'Doc.'" She set her cup down with a snap.

"Fine. Back to the symbolism. You're afraid of losing your pants."

"What?"

"Yup. Who wears the pants, Jane? If you don't have them on, you're naked and vulnerable. You're not in control."

"That is *so* not true. Would you leave the psychology to me, please? It's not your field."

Dom raised his hands, palms up. "Treading on your territory, darlin' Jane? My apologies. After all, I'm not supposed to have any insights. I'm just the beef here—you're the farmer."

Her jaw worked. "I think you should leave now."

"Getting out your cattle prod?"

It sure is tempting. How did the guy make her feel so in the wrong? Especially when she was doing the right thing? She was being ethical, darn it. And fair, too! So why didn't she feel better about it?

20

ARIANNA DUBOSE HAD RESEMBLED a hornet the last time Jane saw her. Today she looked like a rabid bat. She flew into Jane's office at Finesse, swooped down upon her in black dolman sleeves and extended her claws to get a good grip on her neck before she bit down hard.

In those narrow claws she held Dominic's evaluation, and her blood-red lips opened in a snarl to display her pointed teeth. Jane figured she must have used her rearview mirror to wipe her mouth free of foam flecks before entering the building.

"Hello, Arianna. I was expecting you."

"This," hissed the woman, "is *not* what we discussed."

"Please have a seat. Would you like coffee?"

"No. What I would like is to reach an agreement which I thought we'd already settled."

"Arianna—"

"I made you an excellent offer."

"You certainly did, but—"

"You want to play hardball. I'll up the offer by twenty percent. That's it."

"Thank you. I'm flattered. But I have to decline."

Arianna stared at her. "Jane, dear. Are you crazy or just stupid?"

"Neither, thanks. We've just got a lot of commitments for the next two years," Jane lied, "and I can't take on that kind of workload. We're too small."

"Oh, puh-lease. You have no ambition? You don't want to grow? Establish a real name for yourself?"

If only she knew. Jane was ashamed of herself for even considering the Zantyne offer. She had actually come close to selling her soul in the name of money and success. She'd thought about selling out Dominic. That was disgusting.

"Of course I want to grow," she said to Arianna. *How to be diplomatic here?* "But the truth is that I don't think we'd work well together."

Her visitor threw up her hands. "We've been working together just fine. At least until you decided to screw the pooch!"

What exactly does that phrase mean? Jane found the imagery disturbing. And, ahem, she'd bypassed the pooch for the big alpha dog—Dominic. But there was no need to mention that. None at all. She kept her face impassive, her gaze unwavering.

"Fine," said Arianna. "You want to walk away from an amazing offer, then that's your own foolishness. But I need you to rewrite the Sayers report."

Jane took a deep breath. "No."

Arianna's diamonds sparkled dangerously. They

vibrated with anger. Her nostrils flared. "I've already hired his replacement."

"I'm sorry to hear that."

"We had an understanding!"

"No, *you* had an understanding."

"You know damn well that you led me to believe you were on board. You came into my office and admitted that Sayers is difficult!"

"He is when he's angry. He felt railroaded and he was defensive. You set it up that way."

The vice president's eyes narrowed to slits. "Don't *go there* with me, little Miss Muffet."

Miss Muffet? Jane almost laughed.

"You get one more chance. Rewrite this, or I will crush your little two-bit business."

Jane straightened her spine, ran her tongue over her front teeth and raised her brows. She folded her arms across her chest. "My goodness. I'm trembling. Excuse me while I sit on my, uh, *tuffet* to catch my breath." She sat in her leather chair and placed her hands flat on the desk. "Now, I'm quite sure that I didn't just hear you threaten me. Because that would be unprofessional."

"It's not a threat. It's a promise. And don't think I can't do it. You think long and hard before messing with me, Jane O'Toole."

"I'm not 'messing' with you. But I don't respond well to threats. And may I say that during the course of my research I looked into your past, as well as Dominic's. You've had quite an interesting career path."

Arianna froze. "You can't prove one bloody thing."

"No." Jane smiled. "But I sure can connect the dots." She got up and opened her office door, indicating that they were through. Shannon and Lilia were suspiciously close by. Jane looked for any cups they might have been holding to the wall.

"Arianna, have you met my two business partners?"

"No. Nor do I wish to." The woman brushed past them.

Lilia's brows rose. Unfailingly polite, the etiquette consultant still wasn't about to tolerate the snub. "Oh, but we *have* met, Arianna. At the Executive Women's luncheons. Let me show you out."

Shannon was more belligerent and let it slip that she and Lilia had definitely been listening. She put her hands on her hips and called after the two women.

"By the way, Ms. DuBose, you can threaten all you want, but we're not closing anytime this decade. And we're a *three*-bit business, you bitch!"

"I CAN'T BELIEVE YOU SAID THAT, Shannon!" Lilia lectured her later.

"She deserved it. She's got a nerve coming in here and trying to throw her weight and her *bling-bling* around. I'll bet she's even got a diamond through her—"

"Don't say it, Shannon. That's gross."

"Aw, you're no fun. Anyway, I hope she gets mugged and none of the rocks are insured."

"Bad karma," said Jane.

"Poetic justice."

Lilia changed the subject. "We're proud of you, Janey!"

"Why? Because I kissed off the biggest contract we're ever likely to be offered?"

"No. Because you handled her like a pro, you didn't back down and you didn't compromise your integrity. That means a lot."

"Huh. So how'd you hear everything, anyway? Did you guys hunker down near the HVAC vent?"

"Jane, sweetie, give us credit for more dignity than that. We just switched on the intercom at the reception phone. You can eavesdrop brilliantly that way." Lilia smiled, her face all innocence.

"I think you're an undercover agent," Jane said to her. "You wear Prada and Chanel, yet you can probably kill people with your bare, French-manicured hands."

Lilia's smile widened. "No. But I did take a self-defense class in college. And I once used my hardcover copy of Emily Post to rack a date when he got a little too aggressive."

Jane choked.

Shannon cheered.

Lilia smoothed a nonexistent wrinkle out of her sleeve. "See? I was born to be an etiquette consultant. I'll teach manners by force when necessary. Now, I think we should all have champagne tonight—to celebrate getting rid of the charming Madame DuBose."

DOMINIC WHISTLED AS HE MADE his way to the office of Arianna DuBose. She'd called him in for a chat.

Jane's words the other night had reassured him that he had nothing to worry about. He couldn't wait to watch the diamond-studded old crow eat…crow. And hell, cannibalism suited her to a T.

She sat behind her massive walnut desk, visible only from the waist up. Her severe black hair and pale skin made her red lips look even bloodier than usual—as if she'd just raised her head from a fresh kill. Perhaps she had another employee's severed thigh or arm stored in her stainless-steel minifridge?

Dom did a *rat-a-tat-tat* on the surface of her open door.

She barely glanced up. "Dominic." She sighed. "Come in. Shut the door."

He noted two things that he didn't like the looks of. One, an opalescent gleam in her small black eyes. Two, the glossy Finesse press kit on her desk.

"Have a seat," Arianna ordered him. She opened a file drawer and pulled out an official-looking bound report with a blue cover.

"I'd prefer to stand, if it's all the same to you."

She shrugged. "As you know, Jane O'Toole, the behavioral psychologist who spent some time here, has submitted an evaluation of your personality and performance here at Zantyne."

"Yes, Miss O'Toole and I met and discussed the situation." He played his cards close to his vest.

"Dominic, I'm sorry to say that her report is very disappointing—though not, may I say, a complete surprise to me." She paused. "It can't surprise you, either."

Dominic held himself very still, though shock and betrayal and fury surged from his ears to his heart and pulsed through every vein in his body. He set his jaw and clenched his teeth as she continued.

"Your attitude toward women is perhaps understandable, given your upbringing, but it simply won't fly with me. Since you can't seem to swallow your resentment or control your tendencies toward insubordination and, frankly, chauvinism—"

The jaw he'd clenched fell open at that. "This is complete and utter bullshit!"

"Do not raise your voice to me or use profanity, Mr. Sayers. Both are against clearly stated company policy—"

"I don't believe this!"

"You'd better start believing right now, because you are fired." Arianna stood up. "And don't consider trying to pursue legal action, because I have every incident and warning documented. You've been a trial to work with since the day I transferred here from Chicago and took what you considered to be 'your' promotion. I have tried to work with you, Sayers. I've bent over backward to smooth things over between us, but you just can't take orders from a woman. Top management finally understands, and they are backing me up one hundred percent."

Damn, she was good. She even managed to look pained and wronged at the boorishness and "injustice" of his behavior. He recalled hearing that the best liars were those who convinced themselves first.

"You're a piece of work, woman. Do your lies ever stop? How do you look at yourself in the mirror every day? Christ!" he spat. "I don't think you take a piss without calculating what angle to work, what it will get you."

"Vulgarity and hostility to the end," she noted. "By the way, did I inform you that I'm tape-recording this conversation? Just in case."

He wanted to vomit right on her desk. "No, Arianna, you didn't inform me. Not until you had some good 'attitude' and 'insubordination' documented."

He walked right up to her desk and leaned on it, his face inches from hers. "What makes me sick is how you roped Jane O'Toole into backing you up. What did you offer her? Money? Contacts? A job?"

She didn't blink. "Don't try to physically intimidate me. Back off."

"For the purposes of the tape," Dom bit out, "let me clarify that I am standing on the other side of Vice President DuBose's desk and am no physical threat to her at all."

Arianna's eyes flashed.

Dom continued. "Also for the purposes of the tape, may I conjecture that none of the Connecticut staff nor Ms. O'Toole knows how you got your transfer here from Chicago."

"Don't you dare—"

"You were screwing Blankenship behind his wife's back, Arianna, and you blackmailed him into this promotion!"

"That is complete nonsense—"

"Not to mention the fact that you got the transfer to Chicago after threatening to file a sexual harassment suit against the regional manager in Dallas! Do I need to say more?"

"Get out. Get out, you bastard, or I'll call security."

"I want a copy of this tape. The whole unedited discussion. Understand? And I'm entitled to a copy of that piece of shit report, too."

Arianna lunged for her phone and hit two buttons.

"Oh, no," Dom told her. "I'm leaving peacefully on my own steam. You'd just love to *document* that I had to be forcibly ousted, wouldn't you? I'll have to frustrate you on that score."

Dominic strode to the door and threw it open. He left with one last parting shot. "Just remember, Arianna, that all evil dictatorships end in bloody revolution."

DOMINIC TOLD HIMSELF THAT HE should calm down before confronting Jane, but he didn't anticipate being calm any time in the next month.

All the pieces fit together now—why she'd told him she couldn't see him anymore. It had nothing to do with her ethics! It was because of her lack of them. She'd wanted to sever all ties so that she didn't feel guilty for hanging him out to dry.

Arianna had obviously offered her something in exchange for her cooperation, hence the Finesse PR folder sitting so prominently on her desk.

He simmered with anger at Jane's betrayal. He didn't hate women, damn it, even though after this latest stunt he had a right.

What had gotten into Jane? One night she'd seen stars in his arms, let down her guard, dropped her competitive edge. The next day—it must have been the very next goddamned day!—she'd written up a negative report about him. What had gotten into her? How could she turn on him like that?

He thought about her fear, her need to win and that clinical superiority of hers. He'd left her apartment, and all of those qualities had bubbled right back up to the surface in her. A shower, perhaps a cup of coffee, a good look at a stack of bills…and any feelings for him had fallen by the wayside. She'd been too tempted by whatever Arianna had offered her.

Half in love with her? Was he crazy?

Dom squealed into the parking lot at Finesse and stormed the front door.

He made straight for Jane's office, but the blond amazon who was sprawled on the sofa, filing her nails, stopped him. She did so by raising one of her giraffe legs to the height of his knees. "Is she expecting you?"

Dom looked down at the black-leather-clad leg and spike-heeled boot blocking his way. "No, but she should be."

"She has an appointment right now," said the blonde. "You'll have to wait."

"Do you make a habit to trip clients?"

"Only when necessary." She smiled insolently at him. "Would you like a cup of coffee?"

"No, thank you," he growled. She was stunning—supermodel material—but she left him cold. For one thing, she was far too skinny. Someone needed to go after her with a funnel and a bottle of Hershey's chocolate syrup. For another thing, she was rude. And to top it all off, she was in his way.

She must have decided that he wouldn't break Jane's door down, because she finally removed her leg from his path. "Have a seat." She gestured to the chair opposite the sofa.

He reluctantly did so, though he felt a lot more like pacing the room. Dom folded his arms and glared at Jane's closed door, willing away the schmuck taking up her time.

"Headache?" asked the blonde.

"What? No."

"Tooth pain?"

"No."

"Just garden-variety homicidal tendencies?"

He turned his head toward her. "You certainly make refreshing small talk."

"Thank you. I try. I'm Shannon Shane, one of Jane's partners."

"Dominic Sayers."

"I thought so. You don't look very happy, Dominic."

"I'm not."

"Is there anything I can do to help you until Jane's free?"

"Yep. You can get me a tire iron, a steak knife, a tarp and some rope. Maybe some concrete blocks, too."

"That's not funny."

"You set the tone of this conversation. Now you don't feel comfortable with where it's going?"

Shannon cocked her head and looked at him for a long moment. "I like you, Sayers. I'm not sure why, but I do."

Jane's door opened and a young woman emerged with a Finesse PR folder. The same type that he'd seen on Arianna's desk. Dominic got mad all over again.

The young woman called over her shoulder, "I still can't believe the difference in the way my boss treats me!" And Jane's voice said, "I'm so glad, Lisa." The young woman exited.

Before he could open his mouth, Shannon said to Jane, "You have a visitor."

Jane popped her head out and greeted him with a big smile. "Hi! So you must have gotten the good news."

"A *cranky* visitor," added Shannon, rising from the couch and moving toward her own office. "See ya, Sayers."

Jane looked a question at him. "Cranky? Why? Come in."

He strode past her and turned. The fact that she looked particularly pretty today made him even angrier. He'd trusted her. *Two-faced little psych major.*

"*Why?* Oh, hell, let's see. I enjoy being blind-sided, betrayed and then fired. I think it's fun. What's not to like?"

Jane paled. "Fired? Based on what?"

"*Your report,* sweet Jane. The one you turned in right after you told me that I had nothing to worry about, that I might be surprised. Yeah, I was surprised, don't you know. Surprised right out of my job! Based on your cute little blue report."

Jane shook her head. "I don't understand."

"Nice try. Don't pull the innocent act on me."

"Dominic, the report was positive! I said nothing in it that would give Arianna justification for firing you."

Dom looked at her through slitted eyes. "You lie even better than she does. You play dirty, dirty pool."

21

JANE STARED AT DOMINIC. "Excuse me?"

He walked forward until he almost stepped on her toes, glowering down at her from his superior height. Still absorbing his insult, she didn't back up an inch.

"What did she promise you, Jane? A public endorsement, a big fat fee? Or—" he snapped his fingers "—a consulting contract?"

Jane sucked in a breath as that arrow struck home, and his eyes widened in what he thought was comprehension. Before she had a chance to speak, he overrode her.

"That's it. You *finessed* yourself a consulting contract. Hundreds of thousands of dollars for your new business, without you lifting a finger. All you had to do was *sell me out.*"

She had never seen so much raw contempt on anyone's face. It leaped from his expression like acid and seared her. The fact that it was undeserved made it hurt even more. And despite all of her training, she was only human. She got furious, too. How could he think this of her? How could he? After what they'd shared.

"I didn't sell you out!" she shouted.

He bent forward, lowering his face to an inch from hers. "Spare me your justifications. Don't make me sicker than I already am. You're going to tell me that you didn't make up my background? That I had a bad attitude with you from the start? That I made my own bed, and now I've got to lie in it?"

His hot, angry breath slapped her face with each word. She opened her mouth to hit back, but he continued.

"Did you tell Arianna that *you* were lying in my bed, too? Did you tell her how you came apart in my arms? Did you tell her that *I fell for you*, Jane? That I was half in love?"

His eyes closed in pain and rage, then opened again to focus on her. "Is all of *that* in your *friggin' report?*" he thundered.

Half in love with her? Jane forced a dry, wooden tongue out of her mouth in a futile attempt to moisten her lips. "You don't understand—"

"I understand perfectly. 'Oooh, Dominic,'" he mimicked. "'Thanks ever so for the multiple orgasms! But I've been offered a pile of money to screw you over easy, so don't let the door hit you on the way out.'" He laughed.

"No—"

"Then you used psychobabble on me to justify your exit strategy. All the mumbo jumbo about how our personalities are too unyielding, that we'd never find a compromise, that a relationship between us would never work because neither of us could possibly give up control—"

"Dominic, let me speak!"

"I'm *through* with listening to you speak. You are one sad sack of a woman, General O'Toole. You just go back to manipulating your father, your brother, your cousins. You just retreat to your behavioral psychologist's throne—pass judgement on men for the rest of your lonely life. You'll never be able to share that life with a man until you wake up and decide to respect one!"

Jane felt an almost physical pain in her chest; she found herself unable to speak.

His gaze focused on her mouth, which began to tremble, to her mortification. "I do respect men," she finally whispered.

"No, you don't." His voice was flat and final. "It's the ultimate irony, Jane. You were brought in to judge me for not respecting women. You came on board to fix me or toss me out on my ear. Well, you've tossed me. And I don't need fixing. But I think you do."

Dominic took a last long look at her face. Then he turned and left.

JANE TOOK WOBBLY STEPS backward until her spine hit her office wall. Then she slid down it inch by inch until her bottom rested on the floor. She stared straight ahead at nothing.

Her first conscious thought was that Shannon and Lilia had heard every word without even trying. No cups or intercom eavesdropping necessary. So they knew that she'd slept with a Finesse client…and worse, the part about the multiple orgasms. Shannon would be merciless on that score.

Then she thought about his accusation that she didn't respect men. That hurt. And when she took a good, hard look at herself, the charge held some validity. She'd gone poking into Dom's past, but she'd carefully avoided scrutinizing her own—and what it said about her. Did she insist on mothering her dad and Gilbey because she didn't respect their choices in life? What was this overwhelming need to fix them? Did it stem from a fear of not being able to fix herself? Why did everyone have to be perfect, anyway? Weren't they just as lovable flawed?

It's because I want them to be happy, she told herself. But the truth…the truth was that it was easier to worry about them than to examine her own issues. Like not being able to admit weakness or defeat. Did she have such an ego that she had to control a Jane O'Toole fiefdom? Was that why she scrubbed baseboards with a toothbrush when she got mad? Anger felt out of control to her…so she controlled the dirt in her apartment as a swap?

She'd studied psychology in a desperate bid to understand and control her own emotions. That was understandable in light of her grief over losing her mother. But was it healthy to use her profession in order to curtail the confusion of falling in love?

Admit it, Jane. You couldn't handle the idea of

*being vulnerable to Dominic. Being in love with him
means exposing your underbelly. Being in love with
him means risking loss again—loss and grief. You
helped everyone else get over the loss of Ma. Did you
ever deal with your own devastation?*

Jane sat against the wall for a good hour, vaguely
surprised when Shannon didn't come barging in to
demand the "scoop."

The scoop was that somehow, despite all of her ra-
tionalizations and careful analysis, she had fallen in
love with Dom. She just hadn't been able to admit it
before he did. And now it was too late.

Finally what she should have wondered about *first*
hit her: how had Arianna used her evaluation to fire
Dom when it had been positive?

A nasty, niggling suspicion formed in the back of
her mind. Had the vice president, left with no alternative, rewritten it herself?

JANE EMERGED FROM HER OFFICE prepared to be flayed
by Shannon's acerbic wit. What had she said a couple of weeks before? That Jane had been close to
humping doorknobs since Dom had shown up? She
cringed.

And now both of her business partners had over-
heard intimate details. Her face heated up as she
rounded the corner into the kitchenette for some coffee. She'd rather have a cosmo—or five—but the
clock read only one p.m.

Neither Shannon nor Lilia seemed to be in the office, but on the little tiled table sat a box emblazoned with familiar flowing script, and it smelled like pure heaven. Krispy Kremes!

Jane opened the box and found a note from Shannon inside. "We thought you could use these. One dozen cream-filled, your favorite. Milk in the fridge. Love, S."

Jane's eyes filled with unwelcome tears, and a lump formed in her throat. *Damn it, I am not going to cry.*

She reached for the fattest, most icing-washed doughnut in the box—just to help her swallow the lump. She ate it in three bites and grabbed another while walking to the fridge for the milk. Sugar and vanilla and fat partied on her tongue in mild hysteria before diving down her esophagus, seeking her thighs. Her head swam with the flavors and utterly ignored the protesting squeaks of her conscience.

Funny, but five doughnuts and a quart of milk later, the lump was still there and tears poured down her face in a steady stream.

Jane never cried. She got a little misty-eyed during sad movies or particularly manipulative long-distance telephone commercials, but she did not boo hoo over spilled milk. She generally just mopped it up and got on with life.

Now she was drinking the milk, binge-eating— she undid the top button of her trousers and grabbed yet another doughnut—and sobbing in her office over a *stupid man*. This undignified, destructive behavior was all his fault. And she did, too, respect him.

She respected him enough to strangle him immediately, with her bare, icing-encrusted hands. And after she strangled him for thinking she was such a lowlife, she'd…she'd…

Jane gazed for a long moment at the backward gold script that spelled out F-i-n-e-s-s-e on the glass door. Something crude, unladylike and unprofessional rumbled at the back of her throat. Jane tried as hard to stifle it as she tried to repress her emotions, with equal success. Finally she gave up and emitted an almighty burp.

When Lilia and Shannon walked in a half hour later, she was splayed on the office couch clutching her stomach.

"Murderesses," she moaned.

"Well, if it isn't Little Mary Sunshine," Shannon exclaimed in overly bright tones. "What's the matter, did you eat the whole dozen?"

"Five," Lilia predicted. "She'd be kissing porcelain if she ate them all. And remember, five is her special number."

"I hate you both," said Jane with her eyes closed. "Even though I love you. Thanks."

Shannon called from the kitchen. "No way! She ate *six*. She's getting over her five compulsion. Our Jane is blossoming."

"Then these are appropriate," said Lilia.

A *clonk* sounded in front of Jane—something being put on the coffee table. She reluctantly opened her eyes to see what it was.

Lilia stood there fluffing a flower arrangement. A silk one. Yellow roses.

Jane started to laugh. "You guys are the best."

Lilia held up her hand, palm out. "Wait!" She handed Jane an elaborately wrapped package, tall and skinny with a monstrous shiny gold bow.

Jane's brows rose. "What is this, booze?" She pulled off the bow and tore at the paper, anticipating a nice liter of vodka. They'd make some cosmos right here in the office, she didn't care what time it was.

The box did not contain vodka. Instead it held a spray bottle of silk-plant cleaner.

Lilia smirked at her expression. "I just couldn't give you flowers without a way to dust them."

For the second time that day Jane burst into tears, she couldn't say why. They stemmed from a weird gratitude—a thankfulness that Shannon and Lilia understood her and loved her in spite of her flaws. And maybe a little bit because of them.

As she, the CEO, sat there honking like a goose and leaking like a faucet, Shannon's arms came around her and Lilia stroked her hair. "It'll be okay, Jane. We're going to get to the bottom of all this. That witch obviously forged your report. And we think Dominic loves you almost as much as we do—otherwise he wouldn't be so mad."

22

JANE AIMED A DANGEROUS SMILE at Arianna's assistant, Delores. "Of course I understand that she's busy and can't work me in today. Why don't we look at her schedule for tomorrow."

Delores shifted in her chair, blushed and kept her fingers wrapped around Arianna's appointment book.

This told Jane everything she needed to know: the poor girl had been instructed that Jane be denied access to the vice president.

"Well, uh, Ms. DuBose is booked tomorrow and traveling all next week. And then the next week she's…on vacation."

"Is she?" Jane stared down Delores, who shifted again and began to pick at her cuticles. "Well, then— tell you what. I just need the tiniest moment of her time. I'll wait until her current meeting is over."

Delores gulped. "It's going to be a long one."

"That's quite all right. I brought some paperwork with me and I'll just sit here and work on it until she comes out of her office." Sooner or later, the witch would have to use the ladies' room or leave for lunch.

Outmaneuvered, Delores just blinked at Jane as she made herself comfortable in a chair and dug into her briefcase.

The intercom on the girl's desk beeped, and she picked it up. "Yes, Ms. DuBose? No, ma'am, I haven't had a chance—um, sure. Uh, Ms. DuBose? Jane O'Toole is here to see—yes, ma'am, but she said she only needs a moment of your time and she'd wait…."

Jane got up and strode to the vice president's door.

"Ms. O'Toole! You can't—"

Oh, yes I can. Jane opened the door and walked through to face an outraged, solitary Arianna. Delores came running, but Jane simply shut the door in her face.

Without preamble Jane said, "Dominic Sayers paid me a visit yesterday."

Arianna just glared at her.

"I thought I should tell you that I've sent copies of my evaluation to Zantyne's president, your regional H.R. manager and your national H.R. manager."

"You *what?*"

"I thought I'd spare you the trouble. It's part of Finesse's commitment to customer service to take care of little details like that."

"I never authorized you to do such a thing!"

Jane walked forward and placed her palms flat on Arianna's desk. "And I never authorized *you* to falsify my report and use it to fire Dominic Sayers."

"I don't know what you're talking about."

"Yes, you do. My research and analysis indicated that Sayers is perfectly well-adjusted, despite a rocky past with an unstable mother. It's actually surprising *how* well-adjusted he is. Now, I can only surmise the interaction between you two, but he does not display general indications of chauvinism or hostility toward women. Sayers certainly has a healthy temper when provoked, but I reiterate that it's *healthy*. I suggested in my report that he is a valuable asset to this company—highly intelligent, skilled and well-respected. I recommended that the only action Zantyne might consider taking is a transfer, as you and he do not seem to work well together. At *no point* in my analysis did I suggest he be fired."

"How dare you barge into my office and make these outrageous accusations! Sayers picked a fight with me and quit. I didn't fire him."

"That's not what he told me."

"Then he's a damned liar!"

"Or you are."

"Get out," Arianna snapped.

"I'll be happy to leave when I'm finished. You never thought he'd show up at my office and confront me, did you? You thought he'd just storm out, and I'd never know the truth. Let me warn you, Arianna, that if you have falsified my report, I will take legal action. I will see you in court. And I will not keep quiet about this, either. Do you understand?"

The vice president looked at her with loathing. "I'll ruin you."

"More threats, just like the ones you made at Finesse when I refused to rewrite the evaluation. By the way, Arianna—did I mention that I've been taping this conversation?" Jane pulled a minirecorder out of her purse.

"A copy of the tape goes to Sayers. Other copies can be mailed to Zantyne's president and H.R. people."

Arianna lunged for the recording device, but Jane sidestepped her. "Pull yourself together, Arianna! What are you going to do, mug me in your office, knock me out and throw me in the Connecticut River at midnight?"

Though Arianna looked very much as if she'd love to do all of those things, she dropped into her chair, her mouth working.

"Woman," Jane said to her, "you are an embarrassment to the female sex. Backstabbing and sleeping your way to the top is *soooo* passé. Women do things right these days. They deserve their promotions. They have self-respect. If anyone around here needs behavioral analysis, it's *you*."

She exited Arianna's office for the last time and noticed that the intercom-eavesdropping trick seemed to be well-known. Delores was hunched over her desk grinning like a monkey, and she sure wasn't reading a comic book.

As Jane left the ugly brown Zantyne building for the last time, a weight shifted and toppled from her shoulders. She'd done the right thing and she'd seen it through. Not only had she done right by Dom and

gotten her integrity back, she'd also gotten some revenge against the woman who'd jeopardized it. And
bottom line, it would mean a lot more to her to see
Finesse succeed without a corporate crutch.

BACK IN HER OWN OFFICE JANE made several copies
of both the taped conversation with Arianna and her
report. She sent one set to her attorney. She kept one
for the Finesse files. And she packaged a third set for
Dominic.

Her hand shook as she wrote his name and address
on the mailing envelope.

*Did you tell Arianna how you came apart in my
arms? Did you tell her that I fell for you, Jane? That
I was half in love? Is all of that in your friggin' report?*

*You used psychobabble on me to justify your exit
strategy....*

His words came back to haunt her again as she
slipped the tape and report into the envelope.

*I did. I used my profession to keep my distance and
mask my fear. But I never betrayed you—not the way
you think. I betrayed myself and my own needs...and
I suppose I betrayed the gift of love. I looked it in the
mouth and found the teeth too scary.*

How do I say I'm sorry now? Is it too late?

Should she write him a note, enclose it with
these materials? No! As usual, Jane found it hard
to apologize.

*I'm the injured party here. He thinks I'm snake
enough to sell him out for a consulting contract.*

Jane's chin went up, her shoulders went back and she stapled closed the padded envelope.

This is apology enough. Isn't it?

SHE THOUGHT ABOUT IT AS SHE traveled the aisles of the grocery store with a cart, looking for food to take over to her dad and Gilbey's. For some strange reason, neither of them would be in town on Sunday—their usual family dinner night—so they'd rescheduled it for tonight, Thursday. They'd been very mysterious about it over the phone. Jane smelled news and wondered with a sigh if Gilbey had, amazingly, found another job without her help. She doubted he'd sent out the slides to galleries.

Stop it. You're doing it again. Being superior—and not respecting him. He'll do things in his own time.

Jane tossed two fat yellow onions into the cart, along with enough broccoli to feed three families of four. She'd make her mother's broccoli-cheese casserole and some baked potatoes, and Dad could grill some steak.

From the frozen-food section she added a ready-made apple pie and some nondairy whipped cream. The pie could bake right along with the potatoes.

She arrived at Dad's house to find a strange car in the driveway and two beat-up suitcases of Gilbey's in the front hallway. Even more peculiar, excited conversation and laughter emanated from the kitchen. Gilbey's voice, sounding…animated? And Dad… chuckling? And a woman? What was going on?

"Hi, everyone," she said, walking in and dumping the groceries on the counter. Her eyes went immediately to the handsome woman in her early fifties near the sink. "You didn't tell me we had company."

"You must be Jane!" The woman surged forward and took her hands in her warm ones. "I'm Abigail, a friend of your brother's—and now your father's." She smiled at him.

Jane looked at Dad's face, amazed to find him blushing. "Oh. Nice to meet you, Abigail." Her eyes took in four champagne glasses—on doilies, no less—and a bottle of bubbly in a silver ice bucket. Things had certainly gone upscale around here. Where was the Miller Light?

"What's the occasion?" she asked, unloading her grocery bag.

"Perhaps we should let Gilbey tell you."

Her brother cleared his throat. "Abigail is a gallery director in Boston. I sent her slides of my work. My, uh, sculptures."

"So I came to see them in person. They're spectacular! On the cutting edge…Gilbey is a postmodern, conceptual Joseph-Stella-meets-Charles-Sheeler-in-Fred's-Auto-Garage!"

Jane blinked. Whatever the heck that meant. "He is?" She looked at Gilbey, whose normally dull eyes were bright with pride.

"Yes!" Abigail clapped with enthusiasm. "And we're going to give him his own show. In three months. And I've arranged for him to be an artist in residence at Boston University for the summer, not to mention that he'll be included in Henry Weston's up-coming book on outsider art! Your brother is a genius."

Jane stared at the broccoli, because right now it made more sense to her than Abigail's announce-ment. Then she stared at Gilbey again. He stood straight and tall and his shoulders looked broader somehow.

A smile spread across her face. "All those hours you spent building weird stuff in the barn, and the chaos you caused when you put things together back-ward on the assembly line—it was all for a good cause, huh?"

He nodded.

She threw her arms around him. "I'm so proud of you. Congratulations."

As her father opened the champagne behind them, Gilbey rubbed his gym shoe back and forth across the kitchen tiles. "You're proud of me? I always thought…I kinda thought you didn't respect me."

Jane swallowed. She tightened her arms around him. "Oh, Gil. I guess I didn't understand. I just want you to be happy. I respect you one hundred percent—for following your dream and not letting anyone else dictate how you should live your life. Now *that's* success."

Gilbey hugged her back and kissed her cheek. She felt closer to him than she'd felt in years.

Abigail handed her a glass of champagne, and

they all toasted Gilbey and his continued success as a sculptor.

Nobody said a word to Gil when he carved his baked potato into a perfect pyramid—they were a bit underdone—and his steak into a parallelogram.

Dad actually told jokes all through the meal and gazed at the gallery director when he thought nobody was looking. He was clearly besotted. He made no mention of the weeds in the front walkway, the moles in the lawn or the Jets.

No matter what the outcome with Abigail, Dad seemed to have either gotten help on his own or worked himself out of his depression.

Jane had to respect that, too. She really did.

23

ON HIS THIRD CONSECUTIVE DAY of unemployment Dominic actually found himself carving little mice out of Vermont cheddar for Rusty. He had already re-arranged his sock drawer, vacuumed twice and experienced all the horrors of daytime television.

After an hour of "White-Trash Hermaphrodite Teenagers Who Talk Back to Their Grandparents," his mind had curdled along with his blood.

He'd visited every Internet employment site three times, fielded four phone calls from headhunters and sent out five résumés.

He knew he was losing it when Rusty took one look at his third cheddar mouse, bit the head off and walked away.

"Ingrate!" Dom called after him. He wondered if he should take up knitting or—God forbid—go visit his mother. But no—the sanatorium staff would have to superglue any movable objects to the floor or various shelves and tables because of her tendency to throw things at him. And he didn't want to invest in a new umpire's mask, anyway.

The most exciting aspect of his day was getting the mail, and his ears perked up as he heard the little white-and-blue truck approach his apartment building and bank of postal boxes.

He really had to get a job. This was pathetic. Dom forced himself to wait until the postman had driven off, and then went for the mail.

Inside his box were the usual coupons, a newsmagazine, some bills. And an unexpected package.

Dom frowned at the return address on the padded mailer; the thing had originated with the evil Jane O'Toole.

Had she sent him a kilo of anthrax? Had he left his boxers at her place? He was without a clue. However, he knew he didn't want to think about her, didn't want to open anything from her and couldn't care less if she were hit by a bus. So why wasn't he tossing her infernal package into the Dumpster right behind the mailboxes?

Because he was going to throw it in his fireplace without opening it and toast s'mores over it, that was why. He'd toss a sprig of sage on top, to smoke her spirit out of his life. *Double-crossing little psych major.*

Dom stalked to his fireplace and dropped the package on the hearth. He stomped off to the kitchen for some matches. He marched back to the hearth with destructive intent.

Rusty sprawled shamelessly on his back like a C-list model draped over the hood of a car. The cat squinted at him.

"What?" asked Dom. "I'm not opening that. It's from *her*."

Rusty shifted positions and began to clean something Dom would rather not watch him clean.

"That's disgusting."

Rusty stopped and stared telepathically at him.

Dom stared back. "Hey! I do *not* have my head up my ass. That's very rude." He looked back at the package from Jane.

"Fine. I'll open the thing before I burn it." He ripped at the end of the mailer and pulled out a report with a blue cover—and an audiotape. Dom frowned. Then he walked to his stereo system and popped the tape into the rectangular mouth of the cassette player.

FIFTEEN MINUTES LATER, DOM pumped his fist into the air and then grabbed Rusty and tossed him aloft, to the cat's great disgruntlement. "Yeah! Go, Jane, go!"

He dropped his pet on the sofa, where he bounced—a further affront to feline dignity. "See Jane kick ass!"

The cat glared at him and Dom sobered. "And, uh, see Dick be a Dom. I mean, Dom be a dick. See Dom grovel." He sighed. "Yep. I see a lot of abasement and apologies to Jane in my future. I wasn't very nice to her, was I? But first things first."

He sped to the phone and dialed Arianna's direct line. He got her voice mail, but it didn't matter. "Hi, it's the *healthy, well-adjusted* Dominic Sayers here.

You know, your *highly intelligent, skilled and well-respected, valuable asset* to Zantyne? I just wanted to let you know how much I've enjoyed my three days off, but I'll see you in the office tomorrow. We can talk about my transfer then at your—no, make that *my*—convenience. I'll just bet you're prepared to give me a raise and a positively glowing recommendation, and I surely will appreciate that." Click.

Now he'd better dial the number of the nearest florist and order about five dozen roses….

"JANE, SWEETIE. WE NEED TO talk." Shannon and Lilia both had their hands on their hips and seemed annoyed.

"Hmm?" Jane looked up from her keyboard.

"Both of us really need to pee, and there are *sixty* red roses drowned to death in the toilet bowl. We counted. How long are you planning to leave them there?"

Jane got up. "Oh, sorry. I'll move them to the wastebasket."

"Are they from Dominic?"

"Who?"

"Jane! The man gave you multiple orgasms."

A deep masculine voice joined the chorus. "Yes, he did." Dominic stood in the doorway behind them. "And surely that counts for something?"

Lilia gasped. Shannon laughed.

Jane paled and then did the only thing she could do under the circumstances: she pulled her hair over her face like Cousin Itt. Then she slid under her desk.

"I've got a class to teach," Lilia said quickly. "'Bye."

"And I've got a nerd to make over," Shannon added. "See ya."

Her friends—some friends!—scrammed, leaving Jane to face Dominic's Italian lace-ups. Primo leather. A nice nutmeg-brown. Distinctive stitching down the middle, handcrafted sole…

"Jane, come out from under there," he demanded.

"I don't think so."

"Did you get my flowers?"

"Yup. I watered them well."

"Where are they?"

"You really don't want to know."

"Jane. I need to apologize."

"That's nice."

"It's really hard to apologize to someone who's on all fours under a desk like a dog."

"Yup. Must be pretty rrruff."

"Damn it, Jane." He walked around her desk and leaned down. "Come out. So what if your friends know about the multiple—"

"I can't hear you," Jane sang, her fingers in her ears. "La-la-la-la-la-la-la!"

"That's it." Dominic grabbed her by the ankles and pulled her out, despite her trying to kick out of his grip. Then he straddled her and pulled her hands away from her ears. "Listen to me. I'm sorry. I'm sorry I doubted you and I'm sorry I blew up at you. I'm tempted to say that I'm sorry I ever met you, Jane—"

Her eyes widened.

"—but that's not true. The last time we saw each

other, honey, I admitted that I'd fallen half in love with you. Well, I'm here today to tell you that when I listened to your tape, I fell the rest of the way in love."

"Huh," she managed.

"I had a feeling I was going to have to grovel." He let go of one of her wrists in order to smooth her hair out of her face. "Don't put that finger back in your ear. It's immature—almost more infantile than crawling under your desk."

Jane stuck her chin out. "You had me with 'I'm sorry.' Now you're losing your advantage."

"Honey, I never imagined—though I don't know why not—that Arianna would falsify your report. I was stunned, blindsided, furious. I was hurt. I shouldn't have said the things I said. Can I take them back?"

She gave him a wobbly smile. "Not all of them. You told me a couple of home truths that…well, I needed to hear. Not that I wanted to hear them—but that's different. About respecting the men in my life and not using my profession to avoid my own emotions." She swallowed. "Dom, I owe you an apology, too. I did use my analytical training to try to walk away from whatever's between us. I was so scared. I like to be in control. By the way, get *off* me."

Dom looked deep into her eyes and smiled. "Make me."

She leaned forward and kissed him. His response was a long groan. He got up on his knees, cradled her head in his hands and pushed her down onto her back to deepen the kiss. He didn't seem to notice when they rolled on her initiative and she ended up on top, spread over his body like a human quilt.

"Dom—" she broke the kiss "—I think I'm in love with you, too. But don't tell anyone. It's bad for my image."

"Not a word," he promised, working his way under her sweater. "It'll be our secret."

Too late Jane remembered the intercom at the reception phone. They wouldn't…would they? But with Dom's hands on her bare skin, she couldn't bring herself to care.

"Hey, Jane?" Dom asked a few steamy moments later.

"Mmm?"

"I'm getting a special delivery next week, to celebrate my transfer at Zantyne."

"What kind of special delivery?"

"It's rectangular and green and state-of-the-art. We'll be able to play pool all night long—naked."

"Sounds great," she said and kissed him without a trace of fear. "I'm certainly game…."

* * * * *

Be sure to catch the next story in
THE MAN-HANDLERS *series!*
Read Shannon's story, Unzipped?,
coming from Mills & Boon® Blaze™
in August 2006.

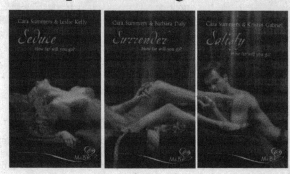

2 FREE

BOOKS AND A SURPRISE GIFT!

We would like to take this opportunity to thank you for reading this Mills & Boon® book by offering you the chance to take TWO more specially selected titles from the Blaze™ series absolutely FREE! We're also making this offer to introduce you to the benefits of the Reader Service™—

- ★ **FREE home delivery**
- ★ **FREE gifts and competitions**
- ★ **FREE monthly Newsletter**
- ★ **Exclusive Reader Service offers**
- ★ **Books available before they're in the shops**

Accepting these FREE books and gift places you under no obligation to buy, you may cancel at any time, even after receiving your free shipment. Simply complete your details below and return the entire page to the address below. You don't even need a stamp!

YES! Please send me 2 free Blaze books and a surprise gift. I understand that unless I hear from me, I will receive 4 superb new titles every month for just £3.10 each, postage and packing free. I am under no obligation to purchase any books and may cancel my subscription at any time. The free books and gift will be mine to keep in any case.

K6ZED

Ms/Mrs/Miss/Mr ....Initials ....
BLOCK CAPITALS PLEASE

Surname ....

Address ....

....

....Postcode...

Send this whole page to:
UK: FREEPOST CN81, Croydon, CR9 3WZ